THE MEMORY
OF TREES

Mick Rooney

Aquarius Communications Publishing
Dublin, Ireland

First published in 2011 by Book Republic, a division
of Maverick House Publishers.

This is a 2nd revised edition.

Aquarius Communications Publishing is an imprint of
TIPM Media Group.
www.tipmmediagroup.com/p/welcome.html

ISBN 978-0-9515916-6-6 (Hardback)
ISBN 978-0-9515916-7-3 (Paperback)

SAUL ROSE FROM THE GROUND, AND
ALTHOUGH HIS EYES WERE OPENED, HE SAW
NOTHING. SO THEY LED HIM BY THE HAND
AND BROUGHT HIM INTO DAMASCUS.

The Bible: Acts 9:1 – 8 English Standard Version
(ESV)

*For all who have supported and travelled on this journey
with me:*

Let each one take a sprig.

For my dad, and for all sons and fathers on their journeys together and apart.

1

The elders and wise men sat in a circle in a small clearing shadowed by the giant trees. Each one slowly closed his eyes and thought about the dreams they had during the night. Though each man's eyes were tightly shut, they could still see the shape, texture and colour of every leafy creature surrounding them. Through their noses, they could still breathe the fresh smell of the forest, and through their ears, they could still hear the wind in the branches of the trees. However, this morning, one of the wise men was not thinking of the trees, nor was he thinking of the dreams he had during the night. He was thinking of his son.

When the men left the clearing and returned to their stone huts, the father could not face his work in the fields, nor could he sleep. Before sunset, one of the wise men came to the father's hut, and the father knew the wise man's words would not be good words, because wise men who become fathers know these things instinctively. The wise man stood at the doorway of the hut and spoke to the father who sat beside a small wood-fire.

"My friend, I saw your son in the mountains today. I think he was in The Palace of Dreams."

The father was silent for some moments. He shut his eyes because he did not want his friend to see his tears. He thought about the many days Carlos had left the hut in the morning and went into the mountains. He could picture his son secretly reading through the many books in The Palace of Dreams, and in his soul, for the first time in his life, he knew the burden knowledge can bring a wise man who is a father.

The wise man saw the darkness in the father's soul, and it made him uneasy and sad to see his friend seated in silence beside the wood-fire.

"My friend, I cannot see your face in the dimness of the hut. Your fire is growing hungry. It is time for you to rise up and feed it."

The wise man turned in the doorway of the hut and shut his eyes. He had seen the father's tears, and he knew the father was thinking about his wife and the memory of trees. The wise man could see the sadness in the father's face like never before.

The boy loved the secrecy of trees, and when the moon rose into the sky, he knew it was late. Each leafy cathedral cast its own shadow in the forest. Above, the canopy of growth protected the boy from the cool wind of the evening, but he knew it also hid the starry ocean of the heavens from him. His instincts guided him in the right direction home to his village. His mind still raced and gushed with adventure and magic. He had been to The Palace of Dreams again.

The boy's imagination was first captivated by The Palace of Dreams after his mother's death. His father had been inconsolable for weeks and their stone hut was endlessly filled with people. The boy felt young, weak and helpless around his father and the wise men of his village. They often talked with his father about The Palace of Dreams, describing it as a place of eternal answers, but the boy did not understand the words the men spoke, or the stories the men wove sitting around the wood-fire. The boy wanted to be wise like the men. He wanted to read all the books they had read in The Palace of Dreams. He wanted to help his father grieve, but he could not. He wanted to go to The Palace of Dreams, but the traditions of his village forbade a young boy to go there, not until he could understand the memory of trees. The boy had never disobeyed his father, or the traditions of his village, but he wanted to help his father, and he believed if he walked for long enough in the forest, the trees would see he was truly good and honest, and they would reveal the memory of trees to him. For weeks his father grieved for his mother, and the boy walked in the forest studying every tree—its size, its shape, the texture of its bark, and the many varieties of leaves and fruit. He visited every tree and knew them like a friend, but they did not reveal the memory of trees to him. Finally, the boy had grown impatient with the trees, and it was only then he had decided to go to The Palace of Dreams in the mountains.

He had not expected to get in so easily. There were neither high walls nor gates surrounding the simple log building. At first, he was a little disappointed, but he had not yet sampled the richness, the beauty, the knowledge in the many volumes of books that lined each wall from floor to roof. He had felt sure that when he read enough, and the time was right, he would go into the forest, and the memory of trees would be revealed to him. The entrance to The Palace of Dreams was never guarded, and though the boy believed he was often seen hiding in the shadows inside the large building by the elders and wise men, he was never disturbed once while he read from the books, nor was he removed. He had started to feel safe there.

When he returned home each day, he continued to see the sadness and loss in his father's heart, but each day passed, and still the trees would not reveal the memory of trees. He felt sure that one day he would be able to tell his father how he understood the memory of trees, and his father would be proud of him, and they would be able to speak of wisdom and the love and memories they shared for the boy's mother. Maybe then, his father would no longer grieve.

The boy was eager to reach home quickly because he knew his father would be worried for his safety. But he also remembered his father's warnings about the dangers in the forest during a heavy rainstorm. The wind alone can snap off the thickest of branches and send them crashing to the forest floor. A sudden rainstorm can unnerve and madden some creatures as they race for cover. He stood for a moment on the trunk of a fallen tree, turned his face into the wind, and listened to the sound of the trees. The evening wind blew fiercely through the canopy of leaves above him. The thickest of branches lower down the tree trunks creaked and strained under the force of their master. His father had taught him to recognise the signs of a violent and sudden rainstorm. He knew he had to find shelter quickly. He searched frantically around his immediate surroundings. He could see an old rotting oak about twenty feet away. The tree was so badly rotted that a large, gaping wound had formed in the thick bough. He ran to the old tree, and while he ran he felt the first ice-cold drops of rain sting his bare back. The opening in the bough afforded him just enough room to squeeze into the cavity. He tucked his knees tight to his chest, closed his eyes, and listened. It was a cold place in the cavity of the tree, but it was safe, and he knew his father would want him to take shelter. Because of this, he felt his father would forgive him for coming home late.

The boy could hear the storm outside. The heavens opened with a thunderous clap. He loved storms because of the fearful yet exhilarating feelings they stirred inside him. He wanted to listen to the sounds it made when it battled with the trees. He felt he understood the strength of the trees. While he pondered this, he grew tired. Finally, he slept soundly and dreamed about The Palace of Dreams.

The boy could see his father walking slowly outside their hut. His head was bowed and the wind blew the dirt about his feet. The storm had taken a long time to pass and the boy had slept for hours. He knew that dawn was not far off. His father had seen his son reach the hut and stand in the doorway, but he continued to walk slowly around, making no effort to greet him. The embers of the wood-fire smouldered and cooled. The boy could not see any trace of flame. He knew this was not good. His father had not slept.

"We must go to the clearing in the forest, Carlos."

His father was standing a few feet away from the hut. He walked over to his father who placed a hand on his shoulder. They began to walk together to the clearing in the forest. The boy's mind was empty because he was sad, and because he understood his father's sadness more than ever before. They reached the clearing and sat together on large boulders. It was starting to get cold. They sat still in silence for some time. The boy looked at his father. He was staring at the trees, and the boy knew his father was thinking about the memory of trees. The boy saw that the storm clouds in the sky were clearing.

"Have you been to The Palace of Dreams?"

"Yes, Father, many times."

"But you know about the traditions of our village?"

"Yes, Father, but I was fascinated by The Palace of Dreams and I wanted to know about the books. I wanted to know wisdom. I wanted you to be proud of me."

The father shook his head and began to stare at the trees again. The wind rustled the leaves around them. The boy was sure his father could hear the sound of the wind on the leaves too. Right then, he wanted his father to turn and look into his eyes, so he might somehow understand the memory of trees.

"Did the others in The Palace of Dreams ever see you when you were there?"

His father spoke without looking at him.

"No, Father. They were too busy reading, and I always hid in the shadows with my book."

His father shifted his weight on the rock and looked into his son's eyes. The boy saw nothing in his father's eyes, except sadness and loss.

"The Palace of Dreams contains every word ever written in this world. The books there are the most important things to our people. They're our words and history. They contain every dream and desire known to man.

His father spoke clearly but louder than was necessary. He often spoke this way when he addressed the other wise men and elders of the village.

"Books are more precious to our people than even the tools we use to complete our daily work; as precious as the bond between a mother and her new-born child, as strong and precious as the love we have for our women, because even a book of stories contains tiny fragments of truths, and truth is at the centre of our universe."

"But Father," interrupted the boy.

He got up from the rock and fell to his knees beside his father. The boy bowed his head because he did not want to see his father turn away from him.

"I couldn't help myself, Father. I had a yearning to know about the books and their stories. I thought they'd help me understand the memory of trees."

The boy began to tremble because he felt his father's grief, and he at once felt the burden of every word he had read in The Palace of Dreams weigh down on his back.

"Father, don't be angry with me, I couldn't control my yearning."

The boy began to sob because he could not feel the touch of his father's hand on his shoulder.

"You know about the sacredness of books among our people. Only the elders and the wise men may go to The Palace of Dreams and read the books of wisdom and knowledge."

The boy continued to bow his head because he sensed his father was not looking away from him anymore, and he was too ashamed to look his father in the face. Though he could not see his father's tears, he could hear him crying, and the boy knew his father was thinking about the memory of trees.

"But Father, I wanted to know the story of our world and our tribe, and I grew wild with excitement when I read about the distant lands and exotic adventures of great men and women."

The boy knew his father was still thinking about the memory of trees, but that he was also listening to the words of his son.

"You can't understand such things, you're only a boy, and you can't know wisdom. Wisdom is not the thread which binds the mind to the heart. When a boy recognises his sins and weaknesses, he comes to his father and seeks forgiveness. You didn't."

"But Father, once I began the stories in the books, I knew I had to finish them. I read the words like a starving man eats scraps of food. I turned the pages of every book madly and quickly to see the journey ahead, the way a farmer hurriedly turns his shovel in the earth before the heavy rains of winter."

"Tell me all the words of all the books you've ever read. Tell me their shape; tell me the sounds they make when one word whispers to the others."

The boy grew more despondent and his heart sank deeply into his chest.

"But Father, you know that not even the wisest men of our village can remember all the words of all the books they ever read. I don't see their shape. I only see the people and places the words create in my head. I hear no sounds, only the rustle of the wind in the trees outside The Palace of Dreams. I read silently in the shadows because I fear I might disturb someone. You shouldn't be angry with me, Father. I can remember how every story ends, where every hidden treasure is buried. I know the answers to many complicated calculations."

The boy looked up to meet his father's eyes. The boy could see no sign of forgiveness. His father grew more agitated after hearing the words of his son.

"When the wise men and the elders read, they read only because the word is written, and great men and women have lived and lied so that the word could be written. We read with a passion for each word as if the words were our sons and daughters, as if we were making love to our wives or lovers. We are together as one when we read, because the words show us the shape and colour and beauty of truth, and truth is at the centre of our universe, not wisdom."

"But Father, I understand the words and their meaning. I understand that a book's first few pages are like the beginning of a journey, and the many pages that follow, bound tightly together by the spine of the book, are the backbone of all humanity. I know the final few pages of a book are the conclusion of a story, when all the paths of the journey merge together joyously like the melodic notes of an orchestra. Father, I believed that with the wisdom I gained in The Palace of Dreams, the memory of trees would be revealed to me, and with this memory, we could share our grief and our loss."

His father looked deeply into his son's eyes and he knew the boy had seen the fragments of truth in every book he had ever read. But his father knew his son had not known that truth is at the centre of the universe.

"My son, there's no beginning and no end to a story or a book. If you read just for the sake of wisdom in this universe, you're a fool, like a man wishing his troubles could fade away with the passing night."

They were both silent for a while, and they both thought of the memory of trees. The boy's father stood up, took his son's hand in his, and gestured him to stand up as well. His father led him into the forest, and the pair walked for a few minutes through the trees before coming to a halt. His father released his hand, and he leant over, so that their eyes were level with each other.

"Carlos, a father should know when to share things with his son, but sometimes this is difficult and painful. When the wise of our people know the pain of grief and loss, when they understand it, when they feel it, they come to the trees, because even though age is no mark of knowledge, trees are older, wiser, and greater than any man or kingdom. They listen to us, they grow with us, but above all, they help us deal with our loss."

The boy looked into his father's eyes, and he could see the same light as the approaching dawn. It was weak to begin with, but it was there.

His father turned and pointed to the tree directly in front of them.

"Carlos, for me, this tree holds the memory of your beautiful mother."

The boy remembered his mother, and when he looked at the tree, he recognised it as the tree he sheltered inside during the storm. He walked over to it and ran his hand along the bark and he saw the rotting cavity in the bough. A piece of the bark broke off in his hand.

"But Father, I don't understand. Why this one? This tree is dead."

His father walked over and put his arms around his son.

"This tree once lived. Though it is now dead, it hides nothing from a wise man. When you needed protection last night from the storm, you came to her, didn't you? She was here for you, and we'll both never forget her for that. It's because of the memory I have placed here. When I tended your mother during her long illness, she became the only thing in my world, and for a time, I believed I knew nothing in this world, only her illness, and nothing more. When the men of our village lose someone precious, they go to the trees and place their memory of that person there. Each tree in the forest can hold a single memory in its lifetime, but it will only ever reveal the memory to those who truly understand the value of memories."

They were quiet together until they sensed the onset of a new day. Before they left the forest, and before the rotting tree was out of sight, the boy spoke to his father again.

"Father, aren't books for learning and knowledge?"

"Yes, they are."

"Then, should the young of our village not read the books of wisdom and knowledge?"

"Yes, they should."

For the first time in his life, the boy knew his father understood the memory of childhood.

Although the boy did not want to leave the tree, he wanted to be with his father, and he felt in his heart he had always known about the memory of trees, but he needed to hear the words from his father.

"Father, what is the memory of trees?"

"Love is the memory of trees."

"What is love?"

"Love is the sap which binds the mind to the heart. Love is the unspoken truth between two lovers."

They walked back to the hut, but the boy was still thinking about his mother's tree in the forest. They lit the small wood-fire and sat together through the dawn. It would soon be warmer outside when the sun rose properly.

"Father, can someone love a tree?"

"Yes, Carlos. Sometimes we can love trees."

The wise men and elders of the village gathered in the clearing by the forest. It was a peaceful morning and the sun was just rising up over the tips of the trees. They seated themselves roughly in a circle and shut their eyes. The dreams of the passing night flowed back to them. Though their eyes were shut, they knew one of the wise men was missing, and so they could not continue.

The father and his son walked to the clearing in the forest. They could see the others had already begun. They reached the clearing and sat down in the circle. One of the elders opened his eyes and saw the boy.

"The boy can't sit with us. He is young and can't understand the things which must always remain unspoken between us."

The others kept their eyes closed. They were thinking about the memory of trees. One wise man, a friend of Carlos' father, was sitting next to the elder who had spoken. He spoke quietly, but firmly.

"The boy should stay."

"Why? He is not yet a man," asked another elder.

"It's because the boy understands the memory of trees."

Soon, they were all silent. Their eyes were closed and they were thinking about the memory of trees again. They continued to keep their eyes closed and remained silent because they understood forgiveness.

The boy opened his eyes for the first time since sitting down. His eyelids were heavy and his eyes a little glassy. He could see all the men before him in deep contemplation, except for his father's friend, who was looking over at the boy. He smiled briefly at Carlos and then bowed his head. Carlos took this to be a good sign. It was good because they both understood that the memory of trees is far greater than the knowledge of trees.

2

Carlos had not wanted morning to come. Normally he delighted in the coolness of the night-time and the beautiful colours of dawn. He would always sleep soundly and easily before rising with the new day. But he had not slept well, and though he dreamt of trees, he had been frightened. He had tried dreaming of the tree that reminded him of his deceased mother, but it hadn't helped.

Today, Carlos would be going to the market alone.

He sat with his father at the fire in the centre of their wooden hut eating some fruit and oatmeal for breakfast. They ate in silence. After their meal, his father smoked slowly on his pipe. Occasionally Carlos would catch his father looking across at him sitting by the doorway of the hut through thin, grey smoke clouds. He could tell his father was still angry with him, but he did not care. He knew that if his father had really wanted

to go with him to the market, he would have explained to the elders of the village the importance
of a father spending time with his only son.

"Father," said Carlos.

"Yes, Carlos."

His father did not look across at him when he
answered. He continued to savour the taste of the
mild tobacco in his pipe.

"Couldn't we go to the market another day? We
could stay overnight in the town. Then, maybe,
on the way home, we can go swimming in the river. It would be like the way we used to go with
the other boys."

"Carlos. Please, enough. You are going to the
market on your own for once. I have important
things to talk to the elders of our village about.
And besides, we need new fishhooks and nets. Do
you want us to go hungry when we use the last of
our hooks?"

Carlos' father stood up abruptly, emptied his
pipe into the fire, and walked out of the hut. He
said nothing to his father when he left. He sat
there sullenly for a while digging his bare feet into the loose sand on the floor. He swore to himself that he would never eat again, and that the
men who fished in the river would have no luck
all day. He got up and fetched his backpack. He
could still feel the knot deep in the hollow of his
stomach that he had felt all through the night. It

would not leave him. Yet, deep down, there was a part of him that did not want it to leave. Carlos could not understand his own sadness.

His father had given him some money the previous evening. Carlos placed it carefully in a green cloth bag, tied it with a lace, and then tied it around his neck. He had never had so much money before. He knew his father must have worked long and hard to save that amount. He swung his backpack over his shoulders and set out from the hut. He remembered to pack some bread and cheese and a canister of water for the journey. He hurried along the pathway through the trees. His father had warned him not to be late because he might miss the only bus going to the market that day.

It was still quite early in the morning and there was nobody but Carlos at the bus stop on the main road. It would be a long journey to the market in Lefkosa. The conditions of the roads were poor and the buses were noisy and old. Most people travelled to the markets and towns by taxi if they could afford the fares, or drove there in their own car or truck. Like the taxis, the buses were privately owned and run. People who lived far away from the major towns and needed to travel regularly to the markets mostly used the buses. An elderly man with a walking cane joined

Carlos at the bus stop. He struggled with a large wooden board with hundreds of metal trinkets tied on to it. Carlos recognised the elderly man. He was a trinket seller who had a small stall in the market. He greeted Carlos without uttering a word, simply placing his hand gently on the boy's shoulder for a moment. Carlos looked up at him.

"Are you off to your stall in the market today?"

"Oh, yes, even someone as old as a mountain has to make some money."

The elderly man shuffled awkwardly on his feet.

"I'm going there too. I've got to buy some hooks and nets for my father."

Carlos clutched the cloth bag full of coins tied around his neck. He thought about what he had just said to the man. It was the first time he had really thought about why he was going to the market. It must have sounded like he was excited and really wanted to go. He did not want the man to think this because he could still feel the knot deep in his stomach. He did not know when the fear of the journey to the market would subside and when he would be able to eat with pleasure again.

In the distance, Carlos could see a cloud of dust rising up from the road through the heat haze. The large, yellow, diesel bus drew closer to the stop. Carlos could sense his spirits lift a little.

He was going to the market for his father to buy some important things. He might even have a travelling companion to talk to on the bus. He had food and water in his backpack and money in his cloth bag. He was going on an adventure, alone.

"Quickly, it's here!"

Carlos was not sure if he was half-excited or half-afraid.

"Yes, of course it's here, boy. Doesn't it always come at this time?"

"Yes, of course," said Carlos.

Carlos helped the elderly seller onto the bus with his large wooden board and trinkets. He did not want to seem foolish in front of the man. They paid their fares and went to find some seats. He carried the wooden board ahead of the elderly seller. He looked to the rear of the bus and saw two available seats where they could sit together. But the elderly seller had already noticed someone he knew, another trinket seller sitting by the window. The seller sat in the single available seat next to his friend. Carlos looked back at the two men already deep in conversation. The bus pulled away from the stop and Carlos found a safe place for the seller's trinket board and an empty seat at the rear of the bus. He sat down and peered out the window. Through the dust clouds, he could see a figure emerging from the trees near the stop. He recognised his father. He watched him disappear into the distance.

Above the noise of the bus engine, he could hear the old trinket seller exchanging market tales and gossip with his friend. He thought about the journey ahead of him. He felt the fear in the pit of his stomach again. He was alone, and when the bus moved farther away from his home, a part of him feared he would never see his father again.

The journey into Lefkosa on the old diesel bus would take about an hour on the narrow, winding roads. There were several other stops along the way and Carlos wondered how he would keep himself amused all that time. Some passengers who got on at the next few stops found themselves standing for most of the journey. Carlos thought about his father again. He would know at every moment today exactly what his father was doing. He was a man of habit. They rose every morning shortly after dawn, washed and ate, and then his father would join the men of the village to read and teach each other about the traditions of their people. In the early afternoon, after Carlos had attended school, he would join his father in the fields, and they tended their crops or went fishing by the river. In the evenings, his father would help him with his studies and then they would speak about the books they had read, or the great men and women of strength and learning. Occasionally his father would speak about Carlos' mother. She had died of a slow and severe illness. He knew it still made his father quite sad, but Carlos would try to get him to talk about the good times the three of them enjoyed together. Carlos grew sad sometimes when he thought about his mother too. When he wanted to be close to the spirit of his mother, he would go to a particular tree in the forest and speak to her. This was a tradition of his people. It was said that a person's spirit can live on in a tree after death, and because his people believed that trees are the greatest and oldest of all living things, it would treasure and nurture a person's memories.

The bus pulled in at a bus stop and several people boarded. He wondered who these people might be leaving behind this morning. Carlos also wondered about the times when people who love each other had to part. And though people did not like parting, they knew they would not always be able to control and understand their destinies, and they would not be able to quench the fire that burns on at the time of parting. When people part for destiny, or a little time, they sometimes have to give the most precious part of themselves, and it is this loss which hurts the most. And though Carlos was still inexperienced in life, he trusted that destiny would always protect and nurture precious things. He was not sure what precious part of himself he had given up when his mother died, but he knew whatever loss he had suffered, it must have been very precious, because it caused him the kind of pain inside he had never known before.

"Why do you look so sad?"

It was the voice of a young girl sitting on the outside seat in front of him. He thought for a moment she was making fun of him. She had a pretty, round face, a slightly speckled nose, and her hair was short and brown. And then Carlos saw her eyes. They were bright and honest eyes, and he knew she cared.

"Because I feel sad inside."

Carlos could feel his heart sink into his stomach. "But why?" asked the young girl.

"I've lost someone."

"Is it your mother?"

"Yes, how did you know?"

The girl turned quickly around in her seat and spoke to a woman sitting next to her. The woman craned her neck over her seat and looked at Carlos.

"Did your mommy not get on the bus with you, young man?"

Carlos looked at her for a moment. He knew she must be the girl's mother.

"Monika says you've lost her."

The girl's mother seemed genuinely concerned.

"No, I mean, she's meeting me when I get to the market."

The woman smiled broadly at Carlos and leaned a little more over her seat.

"I'm sure she'll be there to meet you."

She whispered the words reassuringly to Carlos.

Carlos felt awkward in front of the woman. He was sure the girl would not speak to him again. He was still alone and afraid, but a part of him wondered if good things could come from sad things.

The bus reached the market in the centre of Lefkosa shortly before noon. The sun was high up in the sky and a heat haze rose up from the busy streets. The bus emptied quickly. Most people hurried to the cool shade of the market stalls or the narrow side streets. Carlos spotted a water hydrant and decided to drink all the water from the canister in his backpack. He could then refill it from the hydrant. The water in the canister was a little warm, but Carlos still relished the taste of it as it began to quench his thirst. He emptied the remaining warm water out of the canister and went to the hydrant. He held the canister under the nozzle and pushed down on the heavy lever. It creaked noisily, but only a few drops spilled out. He tried again, but this time no water flowed at all. He felt defeated and annoyed with himself for wasting the warm water in his canister. It was the only water hydrant he knew of in the market, and if he became thirsty later on that day, he would have to buy some from a stall or simply go thirsty. He knew that if his father had been with him he would not have allowed him to waste the water. He sat on a small wall beside the water hydrant for a little while. He belched and felt his bloated stomach with his hand. He had drank far too much and too quickly.

"Has your mommy not come yet?"

It was the woman from the bus. She was standing over him clutching onto her daughter's hand. Carlos was puzzled by the way she spoke to him. He was at least a year or two older than her daughter was. He thought she must be used to speaking to younger children.

"I'm alone in the market today. I'm here to buy hooks and nets for my father."

He stood up and readjusted his backpack.

"I've enough money to look after myself for the whole day."

"But isn't your mother meeting you?"

"No. I just made that up on the bus."

He could sense the woman was put off by his manner and she turned and left with her daughter without saying another word. He watched them go through the maze of people in the busy market. The girl's mother would probably tell her daughter how rude he was. And when he saw the girl briefly look back at him, he wondered if she thought he was quite grown up. This made him feel a little better and he tried not to think about the loneliness and sadness he had experienced earlier.

Carlos set about finding a stall where he could buy his father some hooks and nets. He remembered the place he had gone with his father on previous visits to the market, but however hard he looked, he could not find the stall through the throng of people. Eventually, under the blaze of the hot sun, he tired and decided to ask some of the other sellers. Fortunately, he chanced upon the elderly trinket seller he had met at the bus stop.

"Ah, if it isn't our little adventurer. What tales have you to tell me of your day so far?"

"None, sir. I'm still looking for a stall where I can buy my father some hooks and nets."

"Oh, you won't find that stall any more. Old Buck who owned the stall passed away over the cold winter. Very sad, such a warm man."

The elderly seller shook his head slightly and ran his bony fingers through his thin hair. Carlos agreed that Old Buck was a warm man. He had sold his father fishing equipment for many years, and Carlos remembered that he had been quite old and frail on their last visit to the market. Carlos felt the knot return to the pit of his stomach. He would have to tell his father about Old Buck when he returned home.

"Are there any other fishing stalls in the market?"

"Oh, no. Old Buck was one in a million. People came from miles away to buy from his stall. Such a warm old man. I don't suppose I'll be around here in this market forever either."

The elderly seller muttered to himself and continued to shake his head. Carlos said goodbye to the seller and turned away, tired and despondent. His father would be disappointed in him, and besides, they would not be able to fish until they got same new hooks and nets. Now, he did not care if he ever got home that day.

"Young man. Come back a moment."

He heard the voice of the seller call after him. He waved to Carlos to come back to his stall. The seller was in the process of lifting a small box up onto his stall table. Carlos went over and peered at the ornate box.

"I always keep a few odds and ends locked away in this box. Now, hooks and nets, you say," said the seller unlocking the lid and opening the box.

"You have some?" asked Carlos.

"Oh, yes, some of my own, but they're expensive. You see, Carlos, a man of my age finds the efforts of fishing too much. I depend solely on what I make from my stall to eat and drink. I don't need these things. And I think I have a decent net somewhere under my stall."

Carlos clutched the cloth bag tied around his neck. He wanted to help the seller, and he felt the seller had done him a good turn. The sun was blazing hot in the sky and he knew if it had not been for the seller, he would have spent the whole day searching for Old Buck's stall in vain.

"How much for the net and hooks?"

"Twelve."

Carlos' heart sank. He knew he didn't have that much in his bag.

"How much did you bring?" asked the seller.

"Just ten."

"They're a good set of hooks, but I suppose there's no use for them hidden away in this box."

The seller took the hooks out of the box and handed them to Carlos. He could not believe his luck. He gave ten coins to the seller and managed to squeeze the net and hooks into his backpack.

He had just two coins left, just enough money to pay for the bus home that day. He said goodbye to the seller and began to walk through the busy streets of the town. The fear he had about the journey to the market subsided inside of him. He felt like he had passed the biggest test of his life, and he longed to see his father and share his triumph. Right then, he thought he understood the importance of compromise and sacrifice, and the rewards it can sometimes bring someone. A part of him wanted to be at home with his father in their small hut at that very instant. He wanted to thank his father for making him go to the market alone. He thought this must be the part of him that longed to be a young man. But he knew another part of him wanted to explore the busy, market of Lefkosa on his own. He knew this part of him was still a boy. And yet, he was happy.

For a while, he was content to wander through the streets without purpose or reason. Each step he took today, though small, had changed him. He looked forward to coming to the market on his own again. But he also knew that a day would come when his father would need him to travel farther, and he would feel as frightened as he had during the previous night and day. For the moment, he would be happy to go to the market for his father, and he did not want this to change for a time. He wanted to enjoy his future visits to the market and the town, and he did not want to think about journeys which would take him farther away from the only person he loved.

Carlos decided to venture into an area of the town he had not been to before with his father. The inns and places to eat exotic foods fascinated him. He vowed that next time he came he would bring enough money to dine in these fine places. This curious boy with his travelling backpack would amuse the tourists who ate there. He grew hungry watching other people eat, so he went and sat by the road to eat his bread and cheese. He sat outside a large ornate building which he thought must be the tallest and most spectacular in Lefkosa. While eating, he noticed the woman and her daughter once again. They were walking toward him carrying some bags and small flowerpots. He hoped they would stop and talk to him. He felt bad about his behaviour earlier. He had been too consumed with the loss of his water to appreciate their concern for him. The pair crossed the street to the doorway of the large building he sat outside.

Carlos called to the woman.

"It's alright, my father sent me into the market for him!"

She stopped at the doorway and let go of her daughter's hand.

"I'm glad someone knows where you are young man?'

"Oh, it's fine. I've been to the market lots of times on my own. I just thought my mother would meet me on the bus this morning. You were kind to ask after me."

The woman forced a little smile and at that fleeting moment Carlos knew the mother understood what it was like to have a young son, full of life and mischief.

"Monika, don't go far away, I won't be long in here. I'm just going to light a candle for someone."

The girl jumped down the three steps leading up to the doorway of the large building and sat next to Carlos. She gripped her bare knees with her arms and hummed for a few moments before speaking to Carlos.

"She goes in there nearly every time we come here."

The girl gestured towards the doorway. Carlos looked at the entrance to the place. He could see a gold engraved plaque on the grey stonework next to two polished, wooden doors. He read the words to himself, *The Lord's House.*

"Does your mother know many rich lords?"

"What? No, no, it's a church, silly."

Carlos felt foolish. The place did not have the appearance of churches he was familiar with. He and his father did not go to churches. They were people of the land, and the land had always been good to them. He thought about The Palace of Dreams. The place was full of books and the elders and wise men of his village allowed him to go there and read many books. He was the youngest allowed to go there and read. He told Monika about The Palace of Dreams and the books he had read. He told her he had read some scriptures and parables in the Bible. Monika listened to him and told him about the things she had read and learnt. Monika told Carlos about the southern coastal town she lived in. Carlos told her that he lived in a hut by a forest, and he told her about his people. He enjoyed telling her about the traditions of the trees in his village, and how there was one particular tree that he believed was a symbol of his love for his mother and how it guarded her spirit. He told her his mother had died a few years before, and for a time he and Monika were silent and sad together. And for the first time in his life, though Carlos was sad for the part of himself he lost when his mother died, the sadness did not feel as overpowering and painful.

Monika stood up and asked Carlos to come inside the church with her. She showed Carlos the pictures that depicted the signs of the cross. The biblical world and the awe of the Lord's House fascinated him. He never dreamed that someone's home could look like this.

Carlos leaned over and whispered into Monika's ear. "Who lives here?"

"I told you, nobody, it's for worship."

"Worship?" enquired Carlos.

"Prayer. They bless people when they're born and when they die. They celebrate Jesus who died for our sins and Holy God too."

Carlos wanted to sit in the wooden seats for a while with Monika. They sat at the end of a long wooden pew near the centre aisle of the church. Carlos loved the silence and the way the occasional sound would echo all through the place. He felt like leaning back and dreaming together with Monika. He was glad he had met her. He leaned back and closed his eyes. He did not look at Monika. He knew she would do the same, because he thought she understood things the way he did.

"Carlos, my young adventurer."

Carlos leapt up suddenly from the pew. He had been dreaming about trees. A tall white-haired man towered over him. He could feel his legs trembling and Monika clutching at his arm.

"Is your father not in the town with you?"

Carlos recognised the tall man. It was Old Buck, the market seller. He knelt down close to Carlos fearing he had startled him.

"Don't you recognise me, Carlos?"

Carlos strained on his words for a second.

"Buck, Buck, I thought, I mean..."

Carlos could not think what to do or say. He thought about what the elderly seller had told him that day, and felt that the few steps he had taken by himself had meant nothing. He felt both defeated and cheated all at once. He thought about the money he had parted with.

"Weren't you in the market today, Buck, on your stall?"

"No, no, not today, it's a feast day. Everyone knows I don't sell on feast days, even that old stubborn father of yours. Is he here?"

Old Buck started to look round at the other seats in the church.

"No, I'm on my own today, Buck."

"That's alright, I won't tell him when I see him next," he said, winking at Carlos.

Old Buck tapped him gently on the shoulder before walking down the centre of the church toward the doors. Carlos slumped back in the wooden pew. He looked at Monika. She looked at him in puzzlement. He was glad she was there with him.

"Who was that, Carlos?"

"Old Buck from the market. He's dead."

It was nice to sit on the bus and appreciate the cool breeze of the early evening. Monika sat next to him holding two small pots of flowers. Her mother managed to end up sitting next to a man carrying a large cage with a young eagle in it. The eagle screeched wildly every time the bus jolted heavily along the road. The man tried to calm the eagle by whistling and pushing small pieces of carrot through the bars of the cage. Carlos leaned across the centre of the bus to see the young eagle better. He had never been so close to one before.

"Is he dangerous?"

"He's a little villain."

The man held out his hand to Carlos and gripped the cage tightly with the other hand. For a moment Carlos thought he was about to greet him with a handshake, until he saw the man's index finger bandaged up.

"If I hadn't looked after this little villain so much, I'd have a good mind to throw him off the nearest cliff when I get into the mountains. This little feathered beggar has the mind of a tiger but the courage of a cat."

"Please don't throw him off a cliff top. He's probably just scared being separated from his mother."

Carlos got up from his seat and peered closer into the cage.

"Ah, he's just a menace. This is the third time I've taken him into the mountains and tried to release him. It's been going on for three whole weeks since I picked him up by the side of the road. I should have just left him there. Want him?"

The man shoved the cage over to Carlos.

"But what can I do with him?"

Before he could do anything, Carlos found himself with the cage sitting on his lap and the young eagle still screeching away.

"Get him to fly off the highest ledge in the mountains you can find. He's got too attached to me, just keeps coming back when I let him out, again and again. I'm sick of it."

The man sat back down in his seat, bolt upright, with his arms tightly folded, staring straight ahead. Carlos looked at Monika sitting next to him. She was giggling away at him.

"You asked for it, silly."

"No I didn't," snapped Carlos.

Carlos wondered how a wild young eagle could possibly become attached to such a grumpy and disagreeable man.

"What's your father going to think when you get home with that scrawny thing?"

Monika continued to giggle at Carlos.

"Shut up, Monika. Stop laughing. I need to think a bit."

She suddenly fell silent, and although he dared not look straight at her in the seat next to him, he could tell she was sulking and staring out the window of the bus. He felt bad. He did not want things to be like this with her. They had talked, laughed, dreamed and played all day, and he did not want things to end this way. He would soon have to get off the bus at his stop and he wanted every moment of his time with her to be joyful.

"Would you help me release the eagle?"

Monika looked at him intently for a few moments. She wanted to be with this boy with all her heart, but she knew they could not be together for now. The bus journey would soon separate them. Carlos would get off at his stop and go into the mountains before nightfall to release the eagle. She and her mother would remain on the bus until they reached their home by the coast. She longed for the journey to begin again, so she might feel the magic and excitement she had felt about Carlos that morning. Now, they were unhappy together, and she knew they would both be even unhappier apart. She would think about Carlos when they were not together, laughing and talking as they had all day, and for a while, this might be enough, but sooner or later, a time would come when her heart would ache to meet him again.

"You know I can't. I have to go with my mother. I know the eagle will fly for you, Carlos. He will put his trust in you. You were old enough to go into the market on your own for your father. The eagle will see your courage and feed on it, and then he will be free and you will be happy again."

He stood at the bus stop for quite a time. He wondered how long Monika had sat by the rear window of the bus staring back at him. He had wanted to say something to her, at least give her some sign, that when they parted, it would not be for good. And while they were apart, he would still think of her and care for his memory of her as if he were caring for Monika herself, and when he dreamed, it would not just be of the trees, but Monika. Carlos remembered a saying the wise men of his village had:

> *A wise man knows each day the sun will rise and set, and though some days seem shorter or longer than others do, all days are equal in time. But the wisest men know that no two days are ever the same, and some are more precious and special in our hearts than others.*

He wondered if he would ever see Monika again, but he knew he would never forget her, or the time he spent with her as long as he lived.

The eagle settled in its cage. He knew it had been the journey that had frightened the eagle. Right then, he knew his father had wanted him to befriend fear. And yet, he also knew he would never quite know fear in the same way again. The light of the day was fading. He hurried up the mountain with the eagle. He knew just the place to let it go.

It took only a few moments to happen; something very wonderful. He removed a small splint tied around the eagle's foot. The injury seemed clean and mended. The eagle immediately hopped over to a ledge without the least bit of encouragement from Carlos, opened its wings, and leapt off the ledge. He watched the glorious little eagle for a while until it disappeared into the approaching darkness of the sky. Carlos could feel something well up inside him. He was crying, but he did not know why the tears had come. He had not wanted the day to end in loss.

He brought the empty cage back home with him to the hut. His father was stoking the burning embers of the fire when he arrived. He dropped the cage at the doorway, took off his backpack, and sat beside him. His father peered out, bemused by the cage at the doorway, but he made no comment about it.

"So my young adventurer returns," his father announced after a minute or two of silence.

"I wasted my water, Father."

"Never mind, it wasn't so warm today, was it?"

"No, not so warm at all. But I think I was tricked by an old seller into buying the hooks and a small net for most of my money."

"Sometimes, Carlos, though there is still a little love left in old men, there is great trickery and devilment too."

Carlos got up and fetched the hooks and the net from his backpack. He handed them to his father by the fire. His father held the net up and inspected it carefully. He placed the hooks in the palm of his hand and also inspected them very closely.

"They're good ones, aren't they, Father?"

"Yes, yes, they're actually very good ones, Carlos. I should know because they're also very like the ones I sold in the market to someone not a few weeks ago. They even have my initials scratched onto them."

His father looked at him for a second and began to laugh out loud. He stood up and put his arms around Carlos.

"I can go back and find the seller, Father."

"I'd rather you tell me about the birdcage you left outside."

He told his father about the man on the bus with the eagle, and that Old Buck was not dead. But his father took the news as if he had been by his side all day.

Later that night, his father allowed him to drink apple wine with him, and they laughed and toasted Old Buck's good health for another year. Later, before Carlos was seized by sleep, he told his father about Monika, and his father was sad for his son. They lay back in their beds and his father talked for a little while to him.

"Every person's heart is surrounded by the shell of an egg. And though the shell of an egg may seem beautiful, but fragile, it is the symbol of all births and beginnings. Every woman wants to nurture the eggshell surrounding a man's heart, but she must also want to nurture the eggshell surrounding her own heart even more, because there always comes a time for two lovers when only one eggshell remains intact. It is usually the woman's eggshell that survives and grows stronger, because a man is sometimes reckless with beautiful and fragile things. When a man is reckless, his judgement suffers, and when a man's judgement suffers, he feels he is nothing, and he is sad, and his sadness continues to eat away at what is left of the eggshell surrounding his heart. A man judges the world with his eyes and he believes his vision is always straight and true. A woman judges the world with her mind's eye, as well as her eyes, and so her judgement is more tempered and true. A man must know the value of the love he feels and is prepared to share, because this is what strengthens the egg-shell surrounding his heart. A man must also accept that he is not whole of himself alone. When a man loves a woman, he shares his love of her with her. He must learn to share his pains as well as his triumphs, and though happiness is inside all men and women, a man is sometimes afraid to seek, afraid to experience, and so he cannot live happily. And because all happiness must end for a time, a man alone is sometimes content to be just a little happy all the time, rather than being very happy only some of the time. In so doing, he risks never seeking the greater eternal happiness inside him."

Carlos' father could see that his son was sleeping. He was not sure if his son heard all of what he had said. But for once, he knew his son would be dreaming of more than just trees tonight.

3

Carlos knew his father was dying. No hand bearing medicine could change the path of his father's journey. This was not the way of his village and the wise men. Nature gives and takes with equal hands, whether with the hands which nurture and give praise for the offerings of the land or the hands which cast great fever and torrent upon our lives.

"It's time, it's time, Carlos."

His father had murmured these words repeatedly throughout a long night of delirium while Carlos cooled his father's brow with water.

Shortly after sunrise, Syam had appeared in the doorway of their hut. He had come at the same time every day of his father's fever.

"Did he speak during the night, Carlos?"

"Not a word, Syam."

"Then the fever is unbearably weakening him. Some of the wise men of the village will come today. You must think of resting or the fever will grip you too. You should go and cleanse and freshen yourself in the waters of the river."

Syam remained in the hut and Carlos walked the banks of the river. He reached a group of women from the village washing clothes by the rocky bank and stopped to drench his face with water. The women chatted and squawked like a small flock of birds bathing in a pool of shallow water. Carlos thought of his mother and the tree in the forest where he knew her spirit was. He needed to be there at that very moment.

He trekked his way up from the river bank high into the forest. He had not been to this part of the forest since his father fell ill with the fever. When he reached the tree he sat down with his shoulder against the trunk and traced his fingers along the contours of the bark. He remembered when he was a young boy and he was able to climb right inside the great hollow in the bow of the tree. Weariness and sleep seized hold of his mind and body and he dreamed of his mother. And in this dream he saw his mother with his father in their hut. They were close and they were joyous in each other's arms. And when Carlos slowly awoke late in the day from his slumber, he knew right then that his father was no longer in their world.

"Carlos, your father has passed on. We sent some of the men of the village to try and find you."

"I'm sorry, Syam. I was amongst the trees. Forgive me."

"We just kept whispering to your father that you had gone to the market and that you would be back very soon."

Carlos could feel the first tear stinging his cheek. Syam had laid his father out with an incense candle burning on either side of his head. The strong sent filled the hut.

"There is no need of water when a spirit passes on, only the waters that cleanse the spirit itself. There can be no sadness in the heavens and upon the earth. Carlos, there can be no sadness in your world."

Syam placed his hand on Carlos' shoulder. He felt the weight of Syam's hand.

"Remember, Carlos, strength through joy."

Carlos turned and left the hut. He did not want to see his lifeless father. The wise men lined up outside, and when Carlos walked past them, each in turn grasped his shoulder for a moment and uttered the same words.

"Strength through joy."

After each utterance Carlos felt the weight of sadness in his heart grow heavier, until finally, it drowned him and he fell to his knees and cried uncontrollably. He did not care what the wise men and elders thought of him right then.

The men moved uneasily around Carlos in the evening twilight. He sat and watched them chatting together in small groups. Every so often one of them would glance across at Carlos perched on a stone wall by the side of the road. He could not see their faces but he could feel their stoic bodies in the stillness of the coming night. And while he appreciated the presence of the men of his village at his time of great loss, it was really the warm presence of his mother that he longed for most. But she went to the trees and the earth many years ago. Now, his father too spirited away in the wind to the same trees.

Carlos remembered the question he had asked his father on the night of his mother's death.

"Father, what is death?"

"Death is just the beginning, Carlos. It is the beginning of the next stage of your spirit's flight back to heaven, a few more earthly moments experienced and enjoyed, and a few more moments passed when the spirit draws you even closer to God. That is all death is...and everything death is about."

In the pleasant wind of that sad night Carlos remembered how he had lain in bed listening to the whispers of the rustling trees outside and he had wondered how close his spirit was to God.

"Carlos, you must make plans for your father's body to return to the earth. The trees will guide and nurture his spirit now."

Syam stood over Carlos. He had been one of his father's closest friends for many years. They both walked across the dirt road to the stone hut where the wise men had gathered that evening. They had come one after the other throughout the day when news had reached the village that his father's condition had worsened. He was the sixth to die of the fever in the village during the year and he would not be the last.

The men of the village had helped Carlos lay his father's body out in The Palace of Eternal Rest. The Palace of Eternal Rest was an open, four-columned stone temple built many hundreds of years ago by nomadic settlers from the east. The building stood on a raised grass plateau surrounded by lush and sprawling poppies and giant orchids. There, his father's body would rest for three days before being moved to its final resting place in the mountains.

It was a clear moonlit night when Carlos returned to the empty hut he had shared with his father. In the light of the fire the hut was bereft of a soul except for Carlos' own. It was as if Carlos' life, with all his memories, had been sucked away in an instant. Without his father with him, he felt nothing, as if he lived in a world without a mirror to reflect the image of himself. He lay down on a blanket he had spread across the floor of the hut. The wise men had insisted on burning his father's bed. Tomorrow would be a new day, another day, but not a day he had ever dreamed of.

On the third day after his father's passing, Syam and four of the wise men joined Carlos to help him carry his father's body from The Palace of Eternal Rest to the nearby mountain cemetery. His father's body had been wrapped in purple and gold-trimmed vestments of silk. There was a water fountain at the top of the stone steps up to The Palace of Eternal Rest. The water in the fountain was used to anoint the bodies and cleanse every visitor's face, hands and feet before they could walk on the sacred floor. This was a sign that all who visit are cleansed before approaching the purity of the passing spirits of the dead. Carlos and the wise men splashed the water from the fountain on themselves with a silver chalice with small holes. There were two other bodies laid out on polished oak boards. Together they carefully lifted his father's body.

"Father; how can any man bear the weight of death, his own and those closest to him?"

"When you finally bear the weight of my earthly carriage and cast it from the poppies and orchids of rest into the open hands of the mountains, you will share the weight of death equally with wisdom and with love by your side. You will use these as the tools to dig my grave and the weight of my death will be no more upon you because my cleansed spirit will soar to be seated beside my father in the heavens. And one day your cleansed spirit, too, will soar as well to be seated next to the heavenly Father:"

They carried his father's body carefully and slowly up the short sand track to the cemetery. The men and women of the village gathered along the edge of the track. The women tossed the petals of poppies onto his father's body while the wise men chanted in prayer with bowed heads. And again Carlos would occasionally feel a hand upon his shoulder and the same words of comfort.

"Strength through joy."

His father's body was placed into the ground and Syam addressed the gathering.

"As the birds soar above us with our departing brother's spirit, we stand stronger together having known and shared in his love and knowledge. May his spirit be lifted and joyous."

The gathering of villagers soon dispersed down the mountain. The cemetery fell silent. Syam remained with Carlos and placed his arm around his shoulder.

"It's still so hard, Syam. I can't feel strength or joy inside me."

"I understand. Your heart is weary from the journey of the past weeks. In time, a great river will run through it. Perhaps, Carlos, you should stay with my family, just for a while. A young man alone in his hut with no close family at a time of loss makes no sense."

"Maybe not, Syam, but thank you. I'd just rather be at home for now."

"Very well. Come, I'll walk there with you."

When they started to walk back down the mountain, Syam pointed across at a lone figure to the far side of the cemetery.

"He's been standing over there on his own for most of the morning. Carlos, do you recognise him?"

"He's too far away to really see."

"Yes, maybe he's just a nomad resting for a while, but he should respect the sanctity of The Palace of Eternal Rest. Should we speak with him Carlos?"

"No, Syam. I don't think he really means any harm."

4

Carlos spotted the old trader, Savier, at the centre of the market. He could see that Savier was gesturing for him to come over to his stall. Carlos slowly walked across the centre of the market to the trader. He jostled his way through the crowds of people. It was as if he were journeying across a treacherous sea against a great wind and current.

"Look, look, Carlos. I have these fine nets, Indian threads. They won't snag or tear easily. Fine, aren't they?"

Savier smiled broadly and stared at Carlos. There was an awkward silence for a moment. Savier nervously fidgeted with a large sack by his feet. He stared at Carlos again.

"You okay, Carlos?"

"Yes, kind of..."

Savier began rooting at the bottom of his sack. "Listen. Tell your father I've some special nets for him, won't you?"

"My father's gone."

It was the first time Carlos had spoken these words with such finality. He felt as if he had sworn a terrible blasphemy in public. As if he had dishonoured his father for the first time in his life.

Savier looked at Carlos and in an instant he saw and felt the boy's pain. And Carlos looked up at Savier and he saw the heart and spirit of a man whose journey in life now meant very little.

"He's gone, Savier."

"Oh...Carlos...I'm so sorry, so very sorry. I knew he wasn't well with a fever, but..."

Savier placed his arms strongly round the boy's trembling body.

"I'm so sorry, Carlos."

He kept saying it over and over and over again as if it were a mantra and it was he who had plunged a dagger into the heart of Carlos' father. Carlos felt a cool teardrop on the nape of his neck. Savier pushed Carlos from him uneasily, still tightly clutching the boy's hands in his.

"Forgive me. I'm so sorry. It is your *heart* which weighs heavy. I meant to visit him when I heard he was ill."

Carlos felt bad for everyone after his father's death; bad for the men of the village, bad for old Savier in the market, and bad for his father.

I'm sorry, Father, for all my sins, sorry that the world is not the image in your sacred eyes. Sorry for all the wrongs you had to right. I'm sorry that I may not have been all things to you, in your perfect image, but you see, Father, I'm not you. I'm beautiful but imperfect. If I was not the strength of the great trees of the forest or the passion of the fires we light, then at least I have listened and stood quietly with these trees and lit these fires. And at least I moved toward the light of the fires and sought solace in their flames. I respected the fire and the knowledge of the trees. But you must also know that here in our village and in my life, I stand here, a man like you. I love you, but I'm not you. I have already walked much of the journey with you, laboured and loved and laughed and cried with you. But it is time I let your spirit go on without me. I must stay here, because I'm not you and your journey is not mine to hold and keep like a possession. We all have our own paths to wisdom and freedom and to our final spiritual exaltation. My journey without you is just beginning and I have been set free on my path. I'm frozen with fear; fear of the flow of the river, fear of the heat of the sun on a long road, fear of the knowledge I've learnt and testing it each and every day, fear of myself and of fear itself. Sweet Father, how do I go on?

It was an early autumn morning when Syam came to Carlos' hut. Carlos had only just risen from a night of disturbed slumber. The autumn nights were becoming increasingly cool and the wolves high in the mountains above the forest were moving closer to the village in search of shelter for their young during the cold winter months. They had howled for hours long before the break of dawn.

"Carlos, I need to speak with you as one man to another."

Carlos was leaning across the log fire he had gathered and lit outside. He did not look up at Syam. It had been many months since Syam had come to visit him.

"Carlos, there is a new young family here in the village, upstream. They are greatly in need of shelter. The days are cool and will soon grow short of light. The woman is heavy with a child. You do understand, Carlos? It's only right that the strong and young men amongst us give way to those most deserving. I'm sure your father would have agreed."

The fire had just started to burn deep and red, but Carlos stood up and kicked sand over it until the last flame was quenched.

"Yes, Syam. I will prepare some things for my journey. I understand."

Carlos turned without further word and walked away.

"Then I can fetch the family now, Carlos?"

Carlos heard Syam calling after him but he did not reply. He disappeared inside his hut to gather his things.

The blood of the night soon dissipated and the stream of fire and cloud-dust in Carlos' head settled like a sleepy mist on the mountains. He walked along the road casually, but in his mind, he acknowledged the anger he felt through his whole body toward Syam. He embraced his anger for the last time and let it go. It seemed the braver and wiser thing to do than be filled with anger for the sacrifice of his home to others without fortune. His mind was heavy with thoughts of his journey ahead. He had known this day would finally come.

Where do I belong? Carlos thought to himself. And in an instant a voice echoed in his mind. They were not his words or thoughts. It was as if in a second they had been placed there by another. He mouthed the words echoing in his head quietly.

You belong to each night and its secrets of promise, and each day and its gifts of sparkling desire.

Carlos stopped walking any farther. He looked around him. The road was empty, but he did not feel alone anymore. This ill-seen presence did not comfort him. *What am I thinking? Are these the forgotten words of my father?* Carlos looked around uneasily again.

"Father. Are you with me?"

Carlos could hear his own voice disturbing the cool silence of the night. They were his words but he was sure the words from within him were someone else's voice. In a flash, more words came into his mind and he was sure they were not his.

I am not your father but I will guide you like a father.

Carlos was glad he had left the dust of his village behind. He was going to a place he did not know. But for now, as he waited for a bus, he comforted himself with thoughts of the trees. His mother's tree, its whispers of encouragement, and now his father's tree, a stern, tall oak by the river worn by the years, but still and undefeated. Carlos missed his father so deeply that the weight of this loss was like the bough of a tree in the core of his heart. And the weight of his father's knowledge and experience, his losses, his heartbreaks, his triumphs and joys were now Carlos', and his alone.

"*Do you remember the first snows of winter in the mountains through all the years of my life, Carlos?*"

"*Yes, Father. I played in the snow and tasted each flake as it fell.*"

"*Do you remember the death of a fox cub in a trap by the riverbank?*"

"*Yes, Father. We set him free to run back to the forest.*"

"*Do you remember how my heart leapt when I first set eyes on your mother?*"

"*Yes, Father. How sweet a flower to love.*"

"*Do you remember how I felt when I held her hand?*"

"*Yes, Father. You held it tightly as though you would never let go. I remember all your thoughts, all your feelings as if you were here now, within and a part of my very wholeness. How could I forget these feelings and thoughts? To forget them would be to forget you and this is something I could never do. If I could make a deal with God, I would accept hells' fire and damnation so that you and Mother could live on in this arcane world of earthly delights. But I know that I have not fully learnt and this is not a fortitude I can indulge or trade my soul and spirit in.*"

"*Father, what do men die of?*"

"*Men die of many things. They die from the labours of the land, the luxury and idleness of*" *wealth, but the worst things for a man to die of are the absence of love, companionship, knowledge and the spirit. These absences are worse than the ravages of disease and disability, because without love, companionship, knowledge and the spirit, a man has no strength. He has lived and become nothing."*

"Father, I don't want anyone to die. I don't want to feel the close breath of death again in my life."

"Carlos, death only comes to those who fear it most and don't understand it. To those who embrace it and know it for what it is—death is nothing; birth is something. Carlos, have you ever seen a tree die before your very eyes?"

"No, Father."

"Have you ever believed that a tiny seed tossed to the billowing winds of spring could find an endless home in the soil and grow eternally, flower to seed and seed to flower to spawn the greatest sprawling oak in the forest?"

"Yes, Father."

"And have you ever seen such a tree disappear in the darkness of night?"

"No, Father."

"Then, Carlos, you understand and you have gained the knowledge of life and death combined. They are as one."

Carlos sat on the bus with his head against the window. He felt each bump on the road. Slowly, but surely, his mind drifted like an abandoned ship on the open waters of the ocean. It came to him without warning. It was a name so simple that he swore he had known it before. It was like the name of an old lost friend who had slipped out of his life through natural circumstance. And through the years you forget this person's name, but their very being—all you attach to them— remains close by. You remember the hat they always wore. You remember the smell of their clothes, of their breath...the comfort they brought to you. And in that moment, Carlos knew the name of the person who placed these words in his head. He knew the person who was guiding him. He knew the voice that he had mistook to be the voice of his father. And his eyes opened wide and he mouthed the word that came into his head.

Tass.

And in that moment he knew that Tass would never leave him.

Tass, what am I to do now?

You will do what has to be done and it will be done and you will be greater for it. Come into the light and do not be sad in this world.

And though Carlos had heard the voice of Tass before in his head, it was like these were the first words Tass had spoken directly to him.

Do not be sad in this world.

Tass, why did you come to me?

I have not come to you. I have always been here. It is you who has come to me. You are my child, my father, my mother, my teacher, my world, and I am yours. You have simply embraced the light and the light knows and respects you as if you were light itself. A flame does not burn you—it is the finger guided by ignorance that burns.

As the road stretched out before Carlos, the memory of trees seemed to slip away from his thoughts, and quickly as the day grew shorter, the trees became but a seed in his mind. The stars peered out of a crisp, black sky until the lights of a busy city ahead flashed feverishly before Carlos' eyes. Something started to awake in him, but he knew this was not the kindred spirit he had known through his childhood in the village and market.

"Move along, can't stop here. This is a bus terminus not a high street to browse and shop. Move along there, young man," said an overweight man with a beard.

He wore a peaked cap and a dark uniform with a bright silver badge pinned to his chest. Carlos could see the words on it: *Security Attendant.* He knew the man was proud of this badge. He glared at Carlos again, his eyes about to eat him alive.

"Are you headed for the airport or staying in the city, young sir?"

"I don't know."

"Then you best move along until you decide, eh?"

He placed a hand on Carlos' shoulder and pushed him gently but firmly to his left, away from the bus, muttering to himself, "Vagrants."

Carlos sat on the wall of an office block for a while listening to the sound of the city pass him by. It was a kind of strange music. He could not feel its heart, and although across the street he could see a line of trees in large concrete pots, he did not see them like trees. They were skeletal and frightened, as if petrified by the city itself.

Tass, help me, please.

There is a spirit here, but it comes with knowledge and knowledge can sometimes be like a great, dense book. It can take time to read and understand this book. You need not ponder on the wisdom of a city—only the wisdom of the people who dwell within it. There is great fear and ex- citement in this city but nothing you do not already know or have not felt in your life. There is nothing here for you but the concrete and the skeletal trees that were taken from their natural place. They are like you—they do not belong here and they do not want to be here.

Carlos got up from where he was sitting and walked across to the trees on the other side of the street. He reached out and broke off a sprig of greenery. He placed it in his small bag and turned to leave the city. He could not bear to come here again.

You may take a sprig from the tree but it will not disappear from this concrete city. Even the trees, which disappear from sight, have not truly gone. They remain with us in a different form like the memory of a loved one passed away. The trees, like memories, remain in our mind, because like the trees across this earth, we have helped to plant and nurture them. They will always be with this earth, and like our lost loved ones, they will always return to the earth. They have flourished and grown with mother earth and father sky. But they have also grown beyond it, as we will one day. There is never a death amongst trees. They treasure and keep our memories of the people on this earth. And when a tree does stop its earthly growth, it still continues in a different form, no different than the souls of passing yesterdays. We may choose to cut a tree down, to burn a fire for a family, to provide a roof above our heads, to write our experiences of life upon the paper of wood pulp. We may hew and cultivate tools and weapons from the trees' wooden breast or carve the visions of an artist. But the trees are always with us. They keep us sacred—together.

There are many great books written about the earth and how we are all here. About how we should build our cities, about how we should best grow up in these places, nurture our hearts and minds, how we should explore our world, how we should be fearful of the evils in it, how we should be grateful for all goodness, both mindful, heartfelt and spiritual. Each step we take follows the last footstep, the last imprint of our forefathers and ourselves. But sometimes we take a step forward—it has great significance and meaning—not for its length of stride or daring, or for its foolishness or courage, but for its honesty, its accomplishment, its significance, its will and testimony, that we have tread there, and known and loved and enjoyed. It is a footstep into the unknown, a walk on the moon, a first kiss, a truth uncovered, a birth, a death, your whole being, known. And if you have found this—it is time to move on.

Carlos knew the city was not the place for him. Its sharpness and formality were not the walls he wished to live within. He remembered how the sun would pierce the cracks in the walls of his hut during the long, warm summers. The bright shafts of sunlight would tease him from daybreak until he could resist its pleasure no longer. The fresh air of the new day would embrace him when he rose and ventured outside. He could not refuse its teasing charm by returning to his bed. It would be like turning his back on a loved one. Once he rose on those summer mornings, he knew the day would always be with him. He had to find a place like his home. And though Carlos knew it was the same air and sky above the city, he also knew that there must be places in the world that reflect differently the passions within the heart.

We awake on a cold and rainy morning, but we must still rise. Why do we rise? It is because each morning brings something new. The cold wind and the murky sky above us are not foreboding enemies. We have seen these mornings before. Such things are as recognisable as friends. We have nothing to fear in each new day. The coldness reminds us that we must wrap up warm and eat well before we go on our way. There are those who feel the cold and say, 'This is colder than any morning I have ever known, therefore, I do not know you and you are not my friend. You are my enemy. I shall lie and sleep a little longer, and maybe soon you will be gone from my life and I will not have to know you as an enemy. And because there is an enemy at my door, I shall not venture outside and face the friends and the things I have to face today. Today will simply pass, and I will be happy for its passing, but less one more day of life.'

"Syam, did my father say anything before he died?"

Syam had known Carlos' father since they were young children in the village.

"Carlos, he was sick and feverish for many weeks. At times he made no sense to us and at other times he spoke great truths that only a dying man would dare to speak."

"But Syam, I need to know his last words."

Carlos pleaded with his father's lifelong friend. Syam understood that the boy was ready and that it was only right a boy should know the last words of his father. Syam knew the boy was nearly a man and had been away in the forest with the trees on the day his father had passed away.

"Carlos, there are only the good and great in this world of ours. Your father was a very great man, not just of the earth, but also of the heavens. Yes, he spoke of you in his last breath. Why wouldn't he? You were his entire earthly world. And it pains me to burden you with this..."

Syam began to weep uncontrollably and Carlos placed his arms around him awkwardly. He had never tried to comfort a wise man of the village in such a way before. He felt so small and weak in the company of this weeping mass of knowledge.

"You see, sweet Carlos. Your father lived and died for you...and this is the greatest thing any man can do for his family. He knew you would never truly be a man with him, and he would, in time, burden you. You see, a teacher, and that is what your father was—what we all aspire to become in life—can show you all things, guide you all of his life, but there comes a time when knowledge must be experienced, lived and felt, and to teach what is already known is simply to teach with a mirror. We must break the glass and discard the image of just our experience. When the time came, your father understood his work was done. His sickness was just a gentle reminder to him of this. Just a gentle word from above...enough...time to come home...we are all waiting for you...teacher."

Syam drifted into a long silence with his head bowed.

"But Syam, what were his very last words? I must know."

Syam eventually broke from his long, silent reverie.

"Yes, his last words, Carlos. He did ask for you. 'Is Carlos home from the market? Just tell him I was tired today, and that I was thinking of his mother and the trees. Tell him I will see him again in a little while. He will understand. He is a man.'"

Syam looked deep into Carlos' eyes. Carlos let go of Syam and they stood apart for a moment.

"Carlos, you will see him again. But for now, when you awake in the mornings, you will be alone, but you will know that a day will come when you will see both your father and your mother again."

Carlos found himself travelling again on a bus back through the countryside. The city he had briefly stopped in was far behind him. The day had passed him by and the dark early hours of a new morning crept upon him. He peered out of the bus window. He could barely make out the landscape of the countryside. It was another world outside and the small villages flashed by in an instant like strangers—homeless strangers. And with each new step he took on his journey ahead, he would be a homeless stranger to all who met him.

A jolt from the bus roused Carlos from his contemplation. Peering outside into the approaching dawn, Carlos could just about make out a man standing at the side of the road feverishly waving his hands at the approaching bus. The bus hurtled by the man forcing him to jump back against the bushes. Carlos leapt from his seat and raced to the front of the bus where the driver sat.

"Please, sir, I have to get off here, right this moment."

The driver glared at him, mumbled something, and the bus jerked to a sudden halt. The doors of the bus noisily opened and Carlos stood motionless at the doorway.

"Well, are you getting off here or not?"

Carlos found himself by the side of the road, hardly understanding his burst of impulse on the bus. As the cloud of dust left by the bus settled, he realised that he had left the few belongings he owned in a rolled up canvas sack on the bus seat. He could see the man by the roadside who had tried to halt the bus. He was now sitting down on his upturned suitcase gazing blankly down at the road. Carlos slowly walked toward the man wondering if he should not have been so impulsive and just stayed on the bus to wherever it took him.

The man turned his head slightly towards Carlos without actually looking at him directly, but he was quick to return his gaze to the road. Silence filled the early morning air and Carlos felt awkward, thinking the man would blame him for not getting the driver to hold on. He mustered up his first words of that day.

"Sorry, you see I was sleeping. I don't think the driver saw you until it was too late. Will the next bus be very long?"

The man was thin and haggard and he looked like he had been travelling the roads for quite some time, perhaps all his life. He shifted on his suitcase and for the first time fixed Carlos with a penetrating stare.

"I wasn't waiting for any bus. I was watching out for you. Thought for a while I'd missed you altogether, that maybe you just weren't coming. I've been here two whole days. So where've you been?"

The man was a just a little older than his own father and he stood up and leaned over Carlos fixing on him with two wildly dilated, steel-green eyes.

"What? But I just stopped here because I thought...well, because I..."

Carlos stopped. There were no words or answers. He wished he could just turn and walk across the road and that he would be back at home in his village. And then Carlos thought of what a home was and he thought of his mother and of his father and his heart was heavy and his eyes filled with tears.

"You stopped here because Bakkar's been sick all this while waiting for you with his ass getting numb by the minute from sitting on this old suit-case."

The man stood up and kicked the suitcase over and it fell into the ditch at the side of the road. Carlos went to retrieve the suitcase from the ditch for the man.

"Leave it, Carlos. It's full of nothing but shit, stuff I'd sooner leave in a ditch with the maggots, and besides, we'd have to drag it for miles."

Bakkar had referred to Carlos by his name.

"You know me, sir?"

"Of course I do. You're still your father's son, aren't you? I mean I know I haven't been around since you were a little cherub in your mother's arms, but I got a letter two weeks or so ago from one of the elders in your village. Well, look Car-los, I don't amount to much on this big island, and I never got along much with your father when we grew up—sometimes that's the way it is with brothers—but you're his son, and that's all there is to it. So let's make some tracks into the mountains."

Carlos knew his father had just one other sib-ling, an older brother, but he never recalled meet-ing him, and his father didn't speak much of his family. He knew they had once lived in the village before he was born.

"When did you leave my village, Bakkar?"

"BAKKAR! Obviously your father didn't talk much about me."

Carlos walked slowly with his eyes on the gravel of the road, afraid to ask another question. The pair walked silently for some moments until Bakkar finally snorted out a reply to his question.

"I left the village long ago. It's too long to even bother remembering,"

"So you didn't study with the wise men in our village? My father didn't talk about you. I'm sorry."

Bakkar stopped walking beside Carlos, insisting on being a few steps ahead of him. He walked with a slight stoop, but at that moment he stopped and stood bolt upright, sighed deeply, and stared back at Carlos who had also stopped in his tracks. Bakkar looked annoyed.

"Carlos, I studied day after day, year in, year out with the wise men of your village. But I've studied with other wise men in faraway places too. I've been on my feet across many lands to places you've never even dreamed of. There's a time when a man has to take hold of himself, become his own master, not just putting a roof over his head and food on his table for himself or his family, but master of his own ideas. I'm done with living and thinking in a village. I LIVE IN THE WORLD."

Bakkar roared the last words out into the countryside and he stretched his arms up to the heavens and slowly turned around and around like a dancer. Carlos thought that maybe Bakkar was quite mad, but he already loved him. And at that moment Carlos wanted to live in the world too.

5

Home for Carlos became an old stone tower high up in the mountains that Bakkar had converted into a curious layer of rooms, one upon the other, rising to the very top of the building. A series of wooden ladders connected each room through a central hole in the floors. Each room had just one tiny window leaving the whole tower in a state of permanent semi-darkness without the use of an oil lamp. About twenty cantankerous goats grazed and stalked the nearby land. Bakkar herded the goats and he referred to them as his hairy mountain bandits. This was their home as much as it was Bakkar's home. The sound of their bells tinkled throughout every waking and sleeping hour of the day. Bakkar had a mixture of respect and loathing for these creatures. They had walked the surrounding land far longer than he had. Like many born of the land, Bakkar fished the streams and rivers running through the mountains. He sold their milk yield at the market and it hardly covered the cost of his meagre provisions. But what Bakkar loved most about his goats was when they locked horns. At the sound of the melee outside, he would rush from the tower calling for Carlos to 'come quick and watch the duelling bandits.'

"Ah, yes, Carlos. I've lost more than one or two over the years. But you must savour the moment of battle."

In the first few weeks Carlos spent living with his Uncle Bakkar, they never once spoke about Carlos' father, and Bakkar never mentioned his childhood with his younger brother. It was as if Carlos' father was a completely different man to both of them, like a spurned brother and a curs- ed *Holy Father.*

When Carlos had lived at home in his village, the truth and the answers to all life's mysteries had seemed very close to him, whether it was the words of a book from The Palace of Dreams or the cherished words spoken by his father. It was as if he was at the edge of heaven and all would be slowly revealed to him when he grew older. Yet, here with his Uncle Bakkar, high in the moun- tains, the mystery and uncertainty of all that is learnt in life seemed inappropriate and useless.

Old Bakkar was a man of routine. Each evening he would set out from the tower and trek into the forest that climbs the side of the mountains and return with a large cluster of logs for the iron stove. The smell of smoke from the cooking of fish or meat would fill the whole bottom level of the tower. Bakkar liked to eat and savour his meal in silence and afterwards he would sit outside the tower and try to mimic the sound of the birds resting in the nearby trees. When he came back inside the tower after dark, he would sit under an oil lamp and scribble away in an old green hard-backed journal. From the moment Carlos first cast eyes on Bakkar, he had not considered him a man of words and books, but he discovered that Bakkar had an entire wooden chest filled with these green journals. Although Bakkar did not speak of what he wrote in the journals each night, the intensity and time Bakkar invested in them led Carlos to believe that it must be of great importance. Bakkar was a solitary and private man. He was different to Carlos' father. He never spoke of Carlos' father or recalled fond memories of his childhood. It was as if he was born of the wind itself. And though Carlos knew he had been a man of his village, he was somehow different to the wise men and elders he knew.

One evening, after Bakkar had slammed his journal shut, indicating to the world aloud that his scribbling for the day was complete, Carlos mustered up the courage to ask him what he was writing about.

"Bakkar. What is it you write in the journals every night?"

"History."

Bakkar knelt down and unlocked the chest with a small brass key and returned the journal safely inside. It was as if by uttering this single word, Bakkar expected Carlos to understand everything his uncle had ever written.

"You mean the history of things long ago?"

"History...history!"

Bakkar barked the words out and slammed the chest shut. He pulled a stool over to where Carlos sat by the door. He sat down on the stool and leaned close to Carlos so that his mouth was only an inch from Carlos' ear. He could feel Bakkar's cool breath on his skin and he looked closely at his uncle's worn face and piercing, steel-green eyes.

"It's history, not of what has been, but what's to come.

Bakkar stood up suddenly, knocking over the small stool he sat on. He went to the heavy oak door and opened it. The darkness outside was only disturbed by a few dim lights far in the distance on the mountainside.

"The wolves are close, Carlos. We must be careful to watch over the goats tonight."

Bakkar stepped out into the night. Carlos got up and followed him outside. Bakkar fixed his eyes on the forest to the north of the tower. And then, for the first time that night, Carlos heard the howl of the wolves,

"Are you frightened, Carlos?"

Bakkar looked back at him. Carlos nodded.

Bakkar decided that they would need to build a large log fire to ward off the wolves. The goats themselves sensed the nearby danger and began to move closer to the tower. Bakkar went back inside and emerged again with his axe.

"Come on, Carlos, we'll need much more wood. It could be a long night."

Carlos followed Bakkar to the edge of the forest. Bakkar scanned the trees in the twilight of the night.

"This one's good, not too small and not too big."

Without warning Bakkar took a swing at the tree and an almighty crack filled the still night air. Carlos looked at the trunk of the tree and Bakkar wound himself up for another swing at it. A sharp but small cut exposed the sap and inside of the tree. *Just a gash,* Carlos thought. With ever more venom Bakkar took another swing at the wooden beast. Slowly, but surely, the gash deepened and widened.

"You won't get the better of old Bakkar!"

Bakkar's roar echoed around them. The goats moved more uneasily than ever. Bakkar began to lunge wildly at the trunk of the tree leaving smaller marks above and below the larger cut. Then he dropped the axe and sat on the ground gasping for breath and clutching his chest.

"Are you alright, Bakkar?"

"Yes, yes, just get the axe and finish her off for me."

Carlos lifted the heavy axe in his hands and looked at the large gash in the tree before him. He thought about his mother and father and the memory of trees. Could this tree have been entrusted with a precious memory? Would someone have entrusted a memory to a tree as young as this one? He knew the tree was strong enough to survive even with the savage cuts to its trunk, but he did not want to disappoint Bakkar or risk losing one of the goats to the wolves. He knew that the fire would not burn strong with just a few logs gathered from the forest floor. He felt again the weight of the axe in his hands and the great power it could wield, and for a moment he dared to savour it. He heard Bakkar still gasping and panting for a steady breath behind him. With a rush of blood and anxiety running through his body, Carlos swung the axe at the trunk of the tree. The thud of the impact sent tremors through him. He followed his first blow with a series of quicker blows, but in spite of all of his efforts, he had barely increased the size of the main cut.

"Leave it, Carlos. Go and collect as many branches and logs as you can find on the forest floor. We'll have to do with what we have got."

Carlos turned on his heels and went into the forest. He looked back and saw old Bakkar walk over to the tree and run his hand down along the bark to the cut the axe had made in the trunk. Bakkar slumped back down on the ground with his back and head against the tree, one life supporting the other—the old and the undefeated.

Carlos returned a while later and they lit a small fire and sat uneasily around it eating some bread and milk. They could still hear the sound of the wolves in the mountains around them, but their howls slowly became more distant.

"I'm sorry about the tree, Bakkar."

"You know, Carlos, it's been some time since I cut a whole tree down by myself. I just thought we'd manage it together. This place gets the better of me more often than you might think. Anyhow, we'll manage with what you collected."

"We should get a better axe in the market, Uncle Bakkar."

"Ah, enough of this sorry talk. We'll snare and kill a rabbit in the morning and roast it for the evening on the fire. There's nothing like rabbit meat roasted on an open fire. It's easy pickings when you trap them. A small pocket knife does the trick."

"I'm not much into trapping or hunting, though my father and I did fish a lot."

"A man's got to eat as well as spend all his time thinking, Carlos."

"Maybe, Bakkar...maybe."

Carlos was tired and he went back inside the tower to sleep. Though Bakkar was getting weary and frail, he did not seem to sleep very much. Often he would stay up sitting outside until just before sunrise. And yet, even before Carlos rose from his bed later in the morning, he would hear Bakkar getting up and going outside to feed and check on the goats.

Time seemed to pass slowly while living with his Uncle Bakkar, and as the days, weeks and months passed, Carlos noticed the sprouting of a new bud on a bush, and the migrating birds from the north building their nests in the trees around them. The cool stormy evenings were very slowly giving way to the warmth and comfort of the approaching summer. It had almost turned a full year since Carlos had left his village, and even with the passing of time, Carlos had no wish to return back there. He had turned sixteen during the summer, yet, in his heart, he knew the journey of his life would not end here with Bakkar in the stone tower. And he knew for certain he would not grow old here, and somehow he sensed that despite all his uncle had done for him, Bakkar did not want this for him either.

Carlos could see Bakkar walking up the hill to the tower. He had been down in the valley for most of the morning since he rose from his short slumber. He was awkwardly carrying a large wooden bucket. Every ten paces or so, he would swing the heavy bucket from one hand to the other, spilling a little of the water every time. Bakkar deposited his load with a heavy thud by the door.

"You should've told me we needed water, Bakkar. I'd have gone down to the stream," said Carlos.

"You washed last, yesterday. You should've known," Bakkar glared at Carlos.

"Ah, forget it, boy. I had other things to do down below anyhow."

Bakkar disappeared inside the tower and Carlos stood for a time outside, staring into the bucket of water. Some small flies had already settled on the surface. Carlos scooped the bodies out with his hand and got a wooden board to cover the top of the bucket.

"Bakkar, what will become of me if I remain here?"

Carlos sat down on the side of his bed. Bakkar was busy writing in his journal. It was unusual for him to make an entry in his journal during the day. In fact, Carlos could not recall witnessing this before. Bakkar did not answer Carlos, but instead, he continued to scratch away quickly on the page. For a time, the scratching of pen on paper was the only sound Carlos seemed to hear. He closed his eyes and the sound filled his head completely. It reminded him of the carvers and their blocks of wood in the market, etching away their last finishing strokes on their life's masterpiece. Then, the carver could only watch it over the coming days get pushed inside a hemp bag or rucksack for a few coins, never to be seen again. The creator, left with just the memory of its image, its shape, and the last memory of their sacred hands upon it.

The scratching had stopped. Carlos slowly opened his eyes. Bakkar smiled broadly at him.

"Getting tired of the place and your Uncle Bakkar, eh?"

"No, no, it's just that I feel I need to do something."

"But you do, Carlos. You feed the herd, gather wood, clean, and cook for both of us most of the time. Sometimes you even remember to get us water!"

"Yeh, just sometimes, Bakkar."

"This isn't about water, Carlos, is it?"

Bakkar looked long and hard at Carlos. He snapped closed his journal and set it down carefully in the open chest. Carlos let out a long sigh and lay back on his bed. Bakkar went and stood at the open doorway of the tower.

"You could choose to stay here until your dying years, Carlos. But these mountains and trees will still look the same. New offspring and herds will come and we'll still have to feed them and keep the wolves from our door. We can continue to fish in the fine weather and entertain the odd passing soul who brings us news from other places. You can forget to fetch water from the stream and lie and dream away while your old uncle writes away and doesn't talk for hours on end. But someday, and hopefully for my sake, a long time away, I'll be dust, and maybe you will still be here, Carlos."

Bakkar turned around and looked at Carlos on the bed. Carlos sat up and gripped his knees together with his arms. Bakkar knelt down and pushed his finger gently into Carlos' chest.

"And inside, Carlos, your heart will be as empty as that bucket will be outside."

Bakkar's voice had slowed, almost to the point of a slow drawl. He weighted each word as if he meant each one to become a millstone around Carlos' neck. Carlos remembered how his father spoke to him. It was as if every word was part of a sermon. Bakkar did not speak like his father. He could be blunt and dismissive and it seemed like every word he uttered seemed gritty and hard like hot stones from the depths of the earth.

Carlos could feel his eyes fill with tears, but there was nothing he could say.

"You know when you start out on a journey, your heart is full, but it slowly empties and fills with bitterness and resentment about the way things go—how things don't turn out the way you expect. Like your Uncle Bakkar, you try to write down all that's happened and all that might happen. You twist things around, all the things that have happened in your life with your own written words, trying to record it all, trying to rewrite history, to somehow reinvent things, but you can't change a thing. You plan and you dream and write about the way things should be, about how you think they'll be. Sometimes you just get too wise and clever, and then, one day, you end up like me, and it really doesn't matter anymore. Carlos, you know more than I ever knew at your age. You're smarter, deeper than even your father or anyone twice your years. It's time to share *you* and not just what you know."

Bakkar prodded Carlos again in the chest with his final few words.

"But Bakkar, I felt I had to leave the village to make room for someone new."

"Look, Carlos, you can't leave your life to chance. Not to an empty, pointless bus journey or the meandering path of the open road. You know I was there for you. We didn't meet by chance. But you must still look to your heart. The water in the stream down in the valley won't dance its way up here to the mouths of the herd outside.

When did you last listen to your heart?"

"What?"

Carlos stood up and wiped a few tears from his cheeks.

"Is it that it's stopped speaking or that you're no longer listening?"

"I suppose I'm just not listening, Bakkar, if I'm honest."

"Sounds to me more like you're getting lazy, Carlos."

Bakkar went outside and Carlos stood in the doorway and watched him wander amongst the goats for a while. Carlos studied this man he had known for almost a year. It was as if he had just set eyes upon him for the very first time. He moved amongst the flock stooping awkwardly as if he were a prowling stranger. Yet, over the many months, Carlos understood that Bakkar knew every goat in the herd as if each one was a part of him. He recognised the angry goat, the stubborn goat, the wayward goat and he accepted them, although he might spend a whole afternoon under the blistering sun searching for one on a treacherous mountainside. They were his flock and they knew him, and they trusted in him. And as Carlos looked upon his Uncle Bakkar, he realised that they were all he had. All he had to try to make sense of the world and his own place in it. And though Bakkar was grateful for all the simple things he possessed, he was still sad.

Carlos left Bakkar to his flock and walked up to one of the higher mountain peaks. He lay with the valley spreading out below him.

It came upon him suddenly. It was a rush of energy through his body that he had not experienced for many months. He knew it was time. And though he could think of a thousand reasons why he did not want to go, he knew that it was time to leave. He lay on his back gazing up at the sky above him and the grass around him became his blanket. It kept him safe. The clouds moved across the sky slowly. They were on their way. He did not need to know where they were going. For now, it was enough he knew where he was going. His heart had spoken and he had listened like he had never listened to his heart before.

Bakkar arrived back home late that night, long after Carlos had settled down in his bed. Bakkar moved about the tower uneasily. Finally, he sat on the edge of his bed staring at the stove.

Carlos stirred and watched Bakkar for a few moments in the half-light of the lamp.

"Are you okay, Bakkar?"

"Yes, yes, of course I'm okay, Carlos. It's just my pen. I've left it down somewhere."

Bakkar stood up again and moved around the tower from one place to another barely recognising where he was. He returned to his chest and took out two journals. He sat on the side of the bed for some moments without moving. The fingers of both his hands gripped the blanket on either side of him. As his grip tightened the blanket was pulled slowly from the sides of the bed into two crumpled masses on either side of him. There was a pained expression across Bakkar's face. Carlos wanted to stand up and go over to him, but he hesitated and remained lying in his bed. Bakkar let out a long relieved sigh and his face grew calm and normal again.

"Are you sure you're okay, Bakkar?"

"I'm fine, Carlos...just fine."

"Bakkar, about tomorrow..."

Bakkar shifted in the bed and the two journals he had taken from the chest fell from the edge of the bed to the floor. Carlos got out of bed intending to retrieve them.

"Leave them, Carlos. I'll find the pen tomorrow. Doesn't really matter, it's late anyhow."

Bakkar tossed off his outer clothing, rearranged the blanket, lay back and pulled it over him.

"It's cold tonight. No, maybe just a little cool. Carlos, what you think?"

"Bakkar, about what we talked about earlier. You're right. I have stopped listening to my heart. I've become lazy. This isn't the end of my journey. I'm grateful for what you've done, but I'm still not quite sure why."

"That's the thing when you get to a certain age. It's the same when you are young. You do things just on impulse because something tells you it's right or it makes sense. I'm not sure, Carlos, at least no more than I was the night I waited for your bus to come along the road. I don't know whether I was at the bus stop for you or just out of guilt or duty. I watched the bus you were on pass by several times. You must have travelled around the island over and over again. Maybe it doesn't really matter why I was there and that you got the driver to stop. But I knew I just had to be there, that's all there's to it."

They were silent for a while. Carlos was unsure if Bakkar was asleep or not, so he whispered out in the darkness.

"Bakkar, did you love my father?"

"Yeh, I loved him. I loved that little brother of mine with all my heart."

Carlos had not expected to hear an answer and was a little startled when Bakkar replied so quickly and with such certainty in his voice.

Carlos thought he could hear Bakkar sobbing a little. Carlos appreciated the darkness right at that moment in the tower. He did not want to see Bakkar like this because he felt somehow he would be betraying him, betraying what they had shared together for the past year or so.

"You know something, Carlos? Your father and I used to run like wild cats down the hills towards the river. Your father tried all the time to keep up with his big brother. Sometimes I'd be pulling him along. Sometimes he'd just about keep up. We'd dare each other, holding each other's hands, just to see who'd let go first, and as hard as I'd try to hold on to his, he'd pull his hand free and let me go on ahead down the hill. And boy would I go! And he'd shout after me to slow down, to be careful, but I'd just keep on going. I cracked my ankle right open one summer and that little shit carried me on his shoulders all the way home."

Bakkar shifted round in the bed and Carlos sat up and lit his bedside lamp. He could see Bakkar had his head buried face down in his pillow and was trying to muffle his sobbing. Carlos got up and went to Bakkar's bedside. He knelt down and put his arm around his uncle's shoulders.

"I swear to you, Carlos, I did love him."

"I know, Bakkar, it's okay. I loved him too. Sometimes some people make it so easy to love them."

"Carlo, in the morning..."

Bakkar spun round quickly in the bed and sat bolt upright.

"There're two journals by the side of this bed. I want you to take them. They're yours, not mine, and they belong to you. You understand? I know you're planning to go."

"Yes, I think it's time I did, Bakkar."

"Now, go on, Carlos, get some sleep. You'll need it for tomorrow. Don't mind me."

Carlos went back to his bed but he did not feel like sleeping.

"Bakkar, are you still awake?"

"Yeh, Carlos, of course this old goat's still awake. Are you going in the morning?"

"Yes, but I just wanted to know if it would be alright if I could stay again...you know, another time, for maybe a day or two if I was passing?"

There was silence for a moment and Carlos thought that Bakkar had drifted off to sleep.

"No."

Carlos had not expected Bakkar's abrupt answer.

"But why not, Bakkar? It would only be to check in on you and let you know I was okay too."

"I thought you would understand. It's the same reason it's time for you to go. Remember your journey here on the bus, when I first met you, when I waited for you at the stop. Well, if you ever see me again, by the side of the road, it'll be raining and it'll be night, the road dirty and the air heavy and misty. Go past me. Don't stop for anything. Because if this all does happen again, then you'll have found me like I really am, isolated and afraid to go on, to take the next step. Just pass me by on the bus and let the pools of rain gathered in the potholes splash and drench me to the bone. Sure, we'll meet up again. But not here, mind. Not in this place, not the way we both are. Come on, Carlos, this old uncle of yours is tired. Get some sleep. I'll see you in the morning."

Bakkar turned over in his bed and Carlos left him as he was.

6

When Carlos awoke that morning he felt a little cold. He sat up in his bed and saw that Bakkar's bed was empty. The door of the tower was wide open. He saw a brown parcelled bundle tied with string at the foot of Bakkar's bed. He dressed and went outside where the meadow stretched out before him, empty and silent, but for the distant birds in the trees. The goats were gone.

Carlos ran back into the tower shouting Bakkar's name high above him into the heavens of the stone tower. He scaled several ladders all the way to the top window and looked frantically out. He scanned the nearby mountainside for any sign of Bakkar and the herd, but nothing stirred and all he could see were the trees. He went back down to the bottom of the tower, feeling dejected and alone. He noticed the small brass key still inserted into the lock of Bakkar's wooden chest of journals. It was unusual for Bakkar to leave the key in the lock. Normally his uncle carried it on a chain tied around his neck. He knelt down and carefully turned the key and lifted open the lid of the chest. It was empty except for Bakkar's pen resting on several withered leaves at the bottom. Carlos sat on the edge of his bed in a daze. He could feel the pounding of his heart. The freshness of the morning breeze blew upon his face.

Carlos picked up the brown parcel and placed it on his lap. There were no markings on the outside paper to indicate it was meant for him. He remembered Bakkar's words before they went to sleep the previous night.

"I want you to take them; they're yours, not mine. They belong to you."

He carefully undid the string from the parcel and unfolded the brown paper from around its contents. He turned the two familiar hard-backed journals around in his hands, unsure if he should dare to open them and read the words hidden within. He slowly lifted open the cover on one of the journals to reveal the first page. It was blank. He quickly fanned through the rest of the pages. His heart sank with disappointment, though he was still unsure of what he had really expected to find. The other journal sat by his feet. Carlos did not want to open this one. He did not want to tease himself with the thought that there might be something written in it. But, again, Carlos could hear his heart. He reached down, picked up the other journal, and fanned through more blank pages. The pages blew a cool breeze in his face. It was as if their sterility and emptiness were mocking him. But amid the sterility and emptiness, something dropped to the floor from between the pages. He gazed down at it. It looked like a small, square, blank piece of card, but when he bent down and picked it up, he could feel the glossy smoothness of the underside on his fingertips. It was a photograph, yellowish and frayed from age, but the image it captured was perfectly preserved.

Carlos walked to the doorway of the tower where the light was good. He recognised Bakkar and his father in the photograph. They seemed to be in their teenage years, smiling broadly. Their hair was wet and matted to their foreheads. Bakkar was holding what looked like a fishing rod and another long rod with a net on the end of it. The two had their arms around each other's shoulders. Bakkar stood several inches taller than his father in the photograph. Carlos could make out a lake or river behind them. He wished he could share the joy Bakkar and his father had experienced on that day.

Carlos placed the photograph back into the journal and was startled to see that he had not noticed the first two pages were filled with

Bakkar's familiar handwriting. He was sure the journal had been entirely empty when he had first fanned through it. Carlos sat back down on the bed and began reading the words.

In the beginning, there was reason, and the light shone upon it. The light grew stronger and shone beyond reason. And in the time that followed, there came great contemplation of why things were as they were. And under the intensity of the great light and the uncertainty to its origins, doubt began to grow across the land. And when there is growth in doubt, there comes the inevitable blossoming of doubt. Amid the blossoming of doubt, reason grew weaker, and at every stage of weakness, doubt flourished still farther, until it stretched to every corner of the lands. And there were many who were born and came to know only of an age of doubt, and that reason itself never really existed in the world at all. And eventually, all foundations of belief were built upon doubt, because it had flourished so well and so widely. In this world, built on the foundations of doubt, there could only be great uncertainty. And in uncertainty, fear comes as a stranger and a visi-

tor: It is the fear of what will become of all things created. The world was soon ravaged by fear; and the light, which is always a symbol of hope, grew dimmer; and all within the world had to move closer to the dimming light as its intensity and warmth faltered. And as fear had embraced the uncertainty, it soon embraced the ever-approaching darkness. For now, the light knew it was dying. Racked with fear across the world, growth and all living things fled this impoverished land, because the light knew it could not live in the presence of absolute darkness. And as the light grew weaker still, it could hear the footsteps of darkness approaching. And when the darkness was almost nigh, the light heard the voice of darkness. 'You are becoming like me and soon we shall meet and be as one.' And the moment came when the light met the darkness, but they could no longer tell each other apart. And yet, there was still the dimmest shaft of light remaining where the two met. The darkness caught sight of this shaft of light before it dissipated into the nothingness. With fear still hanging over the lands, the darkness knew because of that faint shaft of light, that there must have been a moment when it was not pure. But with no light, it could not see the image of itself anymore. It had engulfed and swallowed the light and become one with the light. And in this oneness, the darkness knew a contentedness it had never known before. The darkness was no longer troubled, and because it was no longer troubled, it rested, and from the belly of darkness, the light emerged once again. And the light quickly flourished across the land because the darkness was asleep and contented. And when the darkness did awaken, it knew the spirit of the light had been within it and it was pure and still contented and happy to share the time it had in the world of the light. And when the light and darkness learnt to exist in the world harmoniously, all living things returned to the world.

Carlos was bemused and astounded by the words he had read. They meant nothing to him. And yet his heart told him that they meant everything. While Carlos understood why Bakkar had left the blank journal, he did not understand why he had chosen to leave him the journal with these two particular pages of script. He vowed from that day on he would fill those blank sheets of paper with his own history. But what of the words in the journal left to him by Bakkar?

The morning crept on and he found himself perched against the doorway of the tower reading the two pages over and over again. But each successive reading of the words left him no wiser to their meaning and the significance of why Bakkar had left them with him. If only Bakkar was standing by his side—he would give the heavens and earth to know the significance the words would play upon his life, stretched out before him.

He gathered some things together and put them in a backpack. He wanted to travel as lightly as possible, although he had no idea where his journey would take him or how long he would be on the road. He also placed the two journals into his backpack and hitched it around his shoulders. He closed the door of the tower behind him. Again, Carlos scanned the empty meadow in disbelief. He had been at the top tower window many times that morning, but there was no sign of Bakkar and the herd. He could not believe that Bakkar had not wanted to see him before he left in spite of what he had said to Carlos the previous night. But again, he heard his heart, and he knew that this was the way things should be.

He left the meadow and headed for the open road. Every so often Carlos would glance behind him, half expecting to hear the sound of the goat bells carried in the wind and the sight of his uncle signalling to him to wait. But the meadow was still empty each time he looked back and the wind did not carry the faintest sound of a bell.

Carlos decided that before it grew too late he would travel to the market in the capital, Lefkosa. He would pick up anything he might need for his journey ahead, like a good pair of walking shoes and a coat to protect him from the winds if he crossed through the mountains. And the more Carlos began to listen to his heart, the more he knew every journey he had experienced beyond his home village was nothing to the great journey that lay before him. A feeling of anxiety and elation mixed inside him. He walked quickly along the straight road that led to the market. He could feel the weight of the two journals pushing on his back. All the time, he tried to focus on the stones under his feet. It was his way of chasing away the marauding thoughts in his mind. He was still anxious about Old Bakkar and the herd and he felt ashamed that he was a little elated about what lay ahead.

It had been some months since he visited the market square in Lefkosa. Over the years the market had steadily grown, and on each visit, there seemed to be more and more people. The place was full of more tourists than he could ever remember when he was younger. There had been a time when his father first went to the market and he could speak with the men there in a single tongue of dialect. When Carlos started to go with Bakkar, people travelled from across the sea from neighbouring lands, and the market square would be filled with a colourful array of accents and languages. The merchants and stall owners seemed less interested in the wares of the fishermen and the produce of the local villagers. Slowly, but surely, the scent and charm of aromatic herbs and carved trinkets from Asia and Africa had filled the market over time and more overseas merchants travelled from ports several hundred kilometres away. They brought with them an air of worldliness, authority and aggression.

Carlos could see lines of buses on either side of the dirt road which led into the market square. The smell of dust and diesel filled the air. He could already hear the throng of voices and the noise and bustle of traders loading and unloading their trucks. He noticed a truck parked close to the large stone pillars by the square entrance. As he passed by, a small, grey dog barked wildly inside the enclosed cab. It startled him and he stopped for a moment. A blue and white scarf was draped from one side to the other on the windscreen of the truck. Carlos read the words on the scarf. *Bocea Riccos.* He thought it might be a football scarf.

Inside the entrance to Lefkosa market, Carlos could see a crowd of people. He had never seen it so busy. People pushed and shoved their way past each other and he seemed to be the only person standing still. The square thronged with many voices and he could hear the sound of different types of livestock. He wandered without purpose for a while around the various stalls before finally buying a little food, a coat, and some light shoes for the journey ahead of him. He still had a little money left, but he was anxious about how long it would last. When he made his way back towards the market gates, he could see people struggling to pass a herd of goats gathered just outside in the street. Some people were shouting and gesticulating with their fists in the air at an elderly merchant wearing a hat. The goats were getting agitated and some bucked wildly about in the street. Two younger men climbed out of the cab of the truck. It was the same truck with the blue and white scarf. He could see the dog still snarling and barking inside. Carlos stopped with a group of people at the gates of the square. They had gathered to watch and jeer as the two young men struggled to control the goats. Slowly, one by one, they began loading them into the rear of the truck. As the crowd dispersed and the two men loaded the last few goats, Carlos noticed familiar markings on one of the goats which had wandered up to him. He could not believe his eyes. They were Bakkar's herd.

Carlos walked across the street to a small café with a few wooden chairs and tables outside. He sat down, took his backpack off, and placed it by his feet. Two men were in the middle of a game of chess at another table. They did not seem like traders from the market, but were perhaps locals enjoying the cool breeze of the afternoon. They seemed oblivious to the battle on the board in front of them, and instead they talked incessantly about local politics. An elderly, white-haired woman in a plain black dress came out of the café and asked Carlos if he wanted anything. He asked for a glass of cold tea and she disappeared back inside.

Carlos watched the two young men beside the truck. They had loaded all the goats and were talking to an elderly merchant. Carlos assumed that they were the merchant's sons, or maybe his grandsons. Carlos wondered if he should return to the tower and see if he could find Bakkar. He could not understand why Bakkar would sell his whole livelihood—Carlos had no doubt that the goats in the back of the merchant's truck were Bakkar's herd. Carlos felt bad for Bakkar. He hoped that his departure today was not the reason for him selling the herd. Perhaps Bakkar had come to rely on him too much.

The woman in the café returned with Carlos' tea. He sipped it slowly and it refreshed his mind and body a little. Bakkar's goats had distracted him from the anxious thoughts he had about the journey ahead of him. He watched the three men lock up the truck and walk off towards the busy main street of the town. Carlos knew it was time he should be on his way. Through the wooden grills in the side of the truck, he could see the goats peering across at him. He remembered countless nights he and Bakkar had sat up for hours with the goats around a log fire outside the tower with the howls of the wolves in the distance. They kept them safe, and now, Carlos could do nothing more for the goats. He would have helped get them to the market had he known what his uncle had planned to do.

He finished the last drops of his tea which had warmed in the midday sun. It crossed his mind that he might wait a little while longer until most of the traders and stall owners packed up for the day and travelled home. It would soon be late and he might be lucky to hitch a ride with someone leaving Lefkosa. The two men at the table across from him had left leaving their chess pieces still engaged mid-battle. He watched them for a while continue to talk a little farther up the street. He imagined a waitress clearing up to close the café for the night, carefully putting the pieces away in a box. It would be another battle left unfinished.

The market slowly emptied and the line of buses depleted. The throng of the day gave way to a peaceful hum. Carlos daydreamed for a long while. He thought about his mother and his father. He knew that they were gone but that they were with the trees. And their absence no longer brought him to the point of loneliness. His eyes felt heavy and his mind wandered across the land. He drifted through the many small fishing bays and busy ports. Each port was a gateway to another land. Passage from the northern ports led to the lands of an exotic empire, and the blessed lands lay off the eastern coast. Farther across the sea to the west lay the modern metropolis of the world, and the Dark Continent lay off to the south. Yet, his curious mind remained on his island and crept inland to the foot of the Troodos Mountains. He sensed Bakkar would be back at home in the tower scribbling away in his journals. His uncle could sleep soundly tonight. His goats were quite safe.

He became aware that he had drifted off to sleep. He was awakened by the noise of the last line of buses pulling away and leaving the town for the day. The woman of the café came outside and saw Carlos still there. She smiled at him fondly in a way his mother would smile at him when she found him still awake late at night and went back inside. A moment later she came back outside and placed another glass of tea on his table. She refused to take money for it.

"No, no, please, for the travelling young man."

She went inside the café and Carlos never saw her again.

Across the street, the last few people left the market. They returned to the nearby farms, houses, hotels and restaurants across the whole island. Just as Carlos was about to set off, he heard two men arguing a little farther down the street. Their raised voices caught his attention and he stood up from his seat and picked up his backpack. He walked down the street towards the men, out of curiosity, but something made him stop suddenly in his tracks. He could see the two men clearly. It was Syam from his village and his Uncle Bakkar. At one point, Bakkar walked away from Syam and continued walking farther up the street. Syam followed him and they both stopped and began talking intently again. After a while, they embraced each other and left in separate directions. Carlos felt spurned into the wilderness. He wondered what hand Syam had in Bakkar's actions. He had not seen Syam in over a year since he left his home in the village and although he had only seen Bakkar the night before, it was as if he had not seen either of them for many years. They were strangers in his world. And when Carlos' heart spoke, he knew he would not see them again for a very long time, if ever again. It was as if the world and all he had known and trusted in had begun to conspire against him.

He remembered what Bakkar had said when he asked him if it would be alright if he came back to stay with him again.

"Just pass me by on that bus and let the pools of rain gathered in the potholes splash and drench me to the bone."

Carlos felt the weight of cruelty in his heart. And though Carlos knew that even nature could sometimes seem cruel, its intentions were just and for the good of all. An earthly balance would always be restored to the constant battle between growth and decay. But mankind could never understand the power and weight of the sword of cruelty. Its blade is too heavy and unwieldy for any mere mortal to brandish with both conviction and control. Each swing of the sword of cruelty can only bring about death and decay alone. Yet, in that moment, Carlos wished the pools of rain in the potholes would rise up and turn into a wild torrent never seen across this island before. And perhaps the great rains would help wash away his doubts in all those who had tried to help him. For now, the path ahead seemed less an innocent voyage in his life, but instead, a mysterious and troubling shadow on the horizon hiding devious spirits and magicians.

7

The evening was cool and pleasant when Carlos walked the road out of the market and town into the countryside. The sun was beginning to set and he looked across at the Troodos Mountains in the distance and marvelled at the colours of the evening sky. A fiery red cloud hung heavy over the peaks. Carlos could make out the outstretched arms and legs of a great warrior. It was as if he were leaping from the heavens onto the dark blanket of Troodos' earthly bed. In an instant, Carlos decided this was where he should go, high up in the mountain, with his fingertips stretched out to the heavens, almost touching the gates of the kingdom itself. Feeling his spirit elated and the beat of his heart racing within him, his mind cleared of all troubles, and he drew a great breath of air deep into his lungs, held it a moment, treasuring it, and then released it out through his mouth into the oncoming night. He smiled to himself and picked up his pace on the road.

Carlos heard the sound of a heavy vehicle coming up the road behind him. He was dazed by the headlights when he turned around to see and it was only then he realised it was almost dark. He stood in from the road by a small stone wall at the entrance to an olive grove to let the truck pass. But instead of passing by, it came to a halt and a man peered out of the cab. Carlos recognised the man and the truck from the market. He could hear the goats in the trailer stamping awkwardly around.

"Hey, you shouldn't be walking along these narrow roads in the dark."

Carlos struggled to hear what the man had yelled at him from the cab. The truck was old and noisy and plumes of smoked spewed from its exhaust. Carlos hesitantly walked nearer, looking up at the man.

"Are you walking home?"

"Eh, yes, to the Troodos Mountains."

"Where exactly?"

"I'm not sure. I mean I'll know when I get closer up there."

The man who was driving leaned back inside the cab and spoke to two younger men. They spoke in a foreign language and laughed out loud. They seemed in jovial spirits and Carlos

suspected that they had spent some time drinking in one the cafés by the market.

"My boys and I are going south to Limassol to
get the boat with these goats. Maybe we can take
you a little closer to home. Come on, get in,
mountain boy."

The three men shrieked with laughter and the
driver swung the door open and got out. Carlos
climbed inside and sat at the rear of the cab on a
makeshift seat over the engine covering. To his
right on a shelf by the rear window, a dog lay fast
asleep. He could feel the heat of the noisy engine
and noticed the pungent smelt of diesel. The
driver ground the truck into gear and they set off
up the slight incline of the road. The two young
men chatted away to each other and the driver
occasionally glanced back at Carlos perched
above him.

"You okay back there?"

"Sure, I'm fine."

Carlos had to lean slightly forward to avoid his
head hitting the roof of the cab when the truck
hit a bump in the road. He looked out the side
windows but the darkness across the countryside
made it impossible to make anything out. The
headlights of the truck illuminated the road a little way ahead and every so often small wild ani-
mals would dart across their path, barely
avoiding them.

"I'm Ramon, and these are my two sons, Mastaf and Muktu. We're taking these goats back to our farm in Syria."

"You came all this way for the goats?"

"Not exactly. My father has lived here for years and the boys don't get to see him much. We also came here for winter supplies and maybe a few sheep. But we had very good luck at the market today."

"Really, tell me..."

Carlos sat right up in his seat even though his head was pushed firmly against the roof of the cab. He needed to know why Bakkar had sold the goats at the market.

"Well, it was all a little strange. You see, these goats are fine goats, strong, healthy and they should see a good price at any market, enough to keep even a beggar in food for a whole year. But the herdsman at the market gave them to us for no money at all. Crazy or what? He said he simply wanted to be rid of the creatures. Yet, he spent such a time praising their strength and health to us before we left. From the moment I looked into his eyes, I knew he wanted us to have the goats. Many livestock traders would have paid him more than we could have afforded. I suppose it was fate that we should return to Syria with these goats."

"But, Papa, tell the mountain boy about what the crazy herdsman did ask us to do."

"Mastaf...your manners!"

Ramon glared at his son angrily and for a moment the truck wandered onto the stones and gravel at the side of the road.

"You see what you make me do!"

"Sorry, Papa."

The two sons giggled to each other, and with heads bowed, stared down into the darkness of the cab.

"Forgive me...I don't know your name."

"It's Carlos."

"Well, Carlos of the mountains, the herdsman did ask one thing of us. And this was the strangest thing about our encounter with him."

Without warning, Ramon pulled the truck in tightly to the side of the road and stopped. He cut the engine and turned right round in his seat to face Carlos.

"As I've said, we are on our way to Limassol to meet the boat, but there's somewhere we must stop at first. It's a place I've never been to on the island."

Right then, Carlos listened to his heart. And he could see that Ramon was an honest, simple farmer who had travelled from Syria for the good of his family. It was probably a journey he made several times in any given year. Maybe he often travelled with his sons, but sometimes he must have also travelled on his own, perhaps when his sons were younger. These journeys alone must have seemed so much longer and he must have grown weary and dreamed about his family and his home in Syria. But Carlos saw that tonight, Ramon, the simple farmer, was edgy and troubled. Fate had interrupted his journey home. Though the farmer had great luck at the market, and he had a truck full of supplies to carry himself and his family through the winter, as well as a small and healthy herd of goats, he knew for once, fate had struck a price with his very soul. The farmer had grown steadily more uneasy as the night and journey across the island stretched on.

"Carlos, though you are a young man, you must know this great island better than I do, in spite of all the years I've travelled to the markets here. Do you know a place called Tamassos? It's in the centre of the island and I think this road will take us to it."

Carlos recalled the place from books he had read in The Palace of Dreams when he was younger. He remembered that it was an ancient town that had prospered greatly after the discovery of rich and plentiful deposits of copper. It was visited by many powerful ancient leaders and many writers had described the place in books.

But he was sure all that was left of ancient Tamassos were some plundered tombs and derelict ruins on the outskirts of the village of Politico.

"I'm looking for a particular place close to Tamassos. It's a monastic convent and there is something the old herdsman who sold me the goats asked me to do when we reach the place tonight. And I have to say, the more I think about it, the more troubled I've become."

"Shouldn't we just leave it, Papa, and just drive on to the coast to meet the boat? It could bring trouble on us all."

For the first time, Carlos could see that Mastaf had sobered in spirit and become as serious and concerned as his wise father. Perhaps, only now, did Mastaf take seriously the fact that his father was prepared to carry out the wishes of Bakkar the herdsman.

"Mastaf, I've given my word as a man, whatever will be thought of me. Anyhow, getting late, and we cannot afford to reach the boat too late tonight. We still have to load the herd and goods before we set off."

Ramon revved the engine of the truck and picked up speed along the winding road. Though nobody spoke any further, Carlos wanted desperately to ask Ramon what exactly Bakkar had wanted them to do when they reached the convent at Tamassos. After a few more kilometres,

Ramon slowly brought the truck to a halt again. He leaned out of the cab window and then rummaged in his deep trouser pocket.

"What does it say on this piece of paper, Carlos?"

Ramon stretched back and handed Carlos a piece of paper. Carlos took the paper and slowly unfolded it.

"Mastaf, the light...turn the cab light on so the boy can read."

Mastaf reached up and switched on a small, dim light just above his head. Carlos leaned forward in his perched seat at the rear of the cab and brought the paper close to his eyes and the dim flicker of the light.

"A-g-i-o-s, I-r-a-k-l-e-i-d-i-o-s."

Carlos had to spell the two words out because the light was so dim.

"And the other side of the paper, Carlos? It has the name of the monastery where the convent is."

Carlos flipped the paper over and moved so close to the light that the tip of his nose was almost touching the roof of the cab.

"I can see the words clearer now. It's Saint Heracleidius."

"Yes, yes, that's the place. This is it," said Ramon.

Ramon sat back properly in his seat. He pointed out of the window to a sign partly hidden in shrubs at the side of the road. Ramon parked the truck outside the large, iron, black gates of the monastery. They all sat for a moment without saying anything.

"Papa, couldn't we just leave the bag at the gate? Someone from the convent will surely find it by morning, and then no one would think..."

"No, no!"

Ramon snapped back at his son, Mastaf.

"I've told you what's in that bag. Anyone could pass by and take it. Have you no respect for God and for what is sacred?"

"But Papa, we have only the word of the herdsman. Are you going to believe every word a simple herdsman tells you?"

For once Carlos saw that Ramon could not berate his son for interfering. Ramon looked more troubled than ever and Carlos half expected him to relent and agree to leave the bag at the gate and quickly continue on their journey to the south coast.

"No. I have to do this. Give me a hand with the tailgate."

Ramon got out of the truck and they all followed him. The sons pulled the heavy tailgate down and Ramon stood up on it.

"Mastaf, where is the bag?"

"It's at the back on the high shelf."

"Why put it so far back? We'll disturb the herd. After all the trouble we had settling them and getting them in today."

"I'll get it for you, Ramon. I'm good with herds."

"Yes, yes, Carlos. Hop up here then."

Ramon carefully opened the hinged corral gate keeping the goats inside. Carlos slipped between the gap Ramon had left for him. The eyes of the goats glistened in the moonlight. They shuffled on their hooves while Carlos carefully pushed between them. Some lay on the floor of the truck and he had to step over them. He stopped for a moment and whispered under his breath.

"It's okay, Ramon is a good man. He'll take care of you."

"Are you okay in there, Carlos?"

"Yes, Ramon. The goats are tired, but I think they need water."

Ramon could not see Carlos in the darkness of the trailer.

"We can get some here at the convent. I'm sure the nuns won't mind."

Carlos reached the back of the trailer, stretched his arms out, and felt the area immediately in front of him. Just above his head he could feel the underside of the shelf. He ran his hand along the edge until it pushed against something heavy. He could feel a heavy canvas sack. He slid it off the shelf and was surprised by its weight. It hit the floor of the trailer with a thud.

"Carlos, are you okay?"

"Yes, I have it. It's heavy."

He slowly made his way back towards Ramon with the canvas bag.

"Good. I'll take it from you and lift it down, Carlos."

Mastaf and Muktu closed the tailgate back up and stood uneasily beside their father at the side of the road.

"You two, go and wait in the cab."

The two sons quickly obeyed their father. They seemed glad to leave things to their father. Carlos looked at Ramon. He did not want to return to the truck and abandon Ramon by the roadside with the canvas bag. After all, Ramon could have passed Carlos by on the road and he could have been roaming the lonely, winding roads in the darkness for hours. Ramon bent down over the canvas bag by his feet and untied the string holding it closed.

"Carlos. The herdsman from the market who gave me the goats has placed me in a difficult situation. In exchange for the goats he asked only that I give the contents of this bag to the nuns at this monastery. At the time, when he showed me the books in this bag, I thought nothing of it. Before we parted with the herdsman at the market, he explained that the books were of great religious prophecy. I did question why a herdsman would have such rare and valuable books, but by then the goats were loaded onto the truck and I had given him my word that I would carry out his wish. Now, I worry greatly that these books rightly belong to the monastery and they were taken deceitfully from here. Maybe my son is right; the nuns will see us at best as unscrupulous men, or worse, common tricksters and thieves. Should we just leave them at the gate?"

Carlos could see how distressed Ramon was becoming. He wanted to tell him about Bakkar, and how he had watched him for the past year scribble away frantically in those same journals. But Carlos knew he must be sure of his suspicions about the contents of the canvas bag first.

"Can I see the books, Ramon?"

"Yes, of course."

Ramon pulled one of the books from the bag and handed it to Carlos. He recognised it instantly as one of Bakkar's journals. He knelt down and opened the bag fully to reveal the rest of Bakkar's journals. The embossed emblem on each journal cover took on a new significance for Carlos. He traced his fingers over the embossed cover.

"You see, Carlos. It's the same religious cross as the engraving on the pillars of the monastery."

Ramon pointed to the ornate stone pillars on either side of the iron gates. The symbols matched perfectly. Carlos had never paid much attention to this symbol on the journals before. He understood Ramon's fears and could not understand how Bakkar had gotten hold of the journals. Carlos could not believe that Bakkar would have stolen them from the monastery. Anxiety gripped Carlos now. He remembered his backpack in the cab of the truck and the two similar journals that lay inside. He could be looked upon as much a thief as Bakkar, and even Ramon.

"Papa, hurry. We must leave soon."

Mastaf was shouting at them from the cab window.

"He's right, Carlos."

Ramon took the journal from Carlos and quickly put it back inside the bag and tied it up with the string. He walked over to the gate and dropped the bag beside it.

"Come on, Carlos. We have to go."

Ramon got back into the cab of the truck and started the engine. Carlos walked to the cab. Ramon peered out.

"I know someone will take it before morning. I can stay and watch it for you, Ramon."

"No, Carlos. I shouldn't have involved you in this. I assured the herdsman that I would deliver the books to the nuns. Leave them, Carlos. Just go around and get in the other side."

"Ramon, you have taken me far enough. The foot of the Troodos Mountains is only a few kilometres away. Please, go to your boat and give the goats water when you get there."

"Come on, Papa, he'll get us arrested."

"Shut up, Mastaf!"

Ramon revved the engine of the truck and crunched it into gear.

"Thank you, herdsman Carlos."

He reached back inside the cab and hung Carlos' backpack out of the window. Carlos' heart sunk for a few moments. He did not dare to think of what Ramon and his sons would have thought if he had left the backpack in the cab of the truck and they had opened it and discovered the two other journals. He watched the truck disappear into the night.

He walked over to the canvas bag resting by the gate of the monastery and sat down with his back pushed against it. He could see the dark Troodos Mountains rising like unearthly shadows in the night. He would travel through them tomorrow, but for now, he knew he must return the journals safely to the nuns in the monastery. He was puzzled and a little hurt that Bakkar had not trusted him with the journals, and instead, chose to entrust their safe return to Ramon and his sons. He could not believe Bakkar would have stolen them. It was possible he may have come upon them at a market stall. He felt bad that Bakkar had placed Ramon in such a position knowing the journals belonged to the monastery. He clutched the bag close to him, somehow sensing their importance. His mind drifted off and he was soon dreaming about the goats and Ramon and his sons reaching Limassol and loading their supplies and the goats onto the boat. He dreamt of them setting out to sea and the throbbing sound of the boat engine as they made their way back to Syria. Amidst his dreams, he was aware that there was a part of him that resented being left behind with the journals. He too wanted to be on a journey to Syria. He could have helped Ramon on his farm. Bakkar had understood so well how important it was for Carlos to set out and carve his own journey. Yet, here, by the old iron gates of the monastery, he was finishing something which was part of Bakkar's own journey. He had even given Ramon and his sons a reason to leave the journals behind. Carlos opened his eyes and looked into the darkness of the night, and at that moment, he cursed his fate and how he seemed no longer able to guide his own vision and journey.

Carlos heard his heart speak, but he did not want to listen to the words at that moment.

You are becoming selfish and no man learns anything alone when he is on his journey through the world. Fate will be your signpost guiding you away, when necessary, from your own blinkered but unique vision and path.

He thought about the place Ramon had brought him, and as much as he wished to deny his thoughts, he knew that Tamassos was no longer a random place he simply ended up at. He knew he was already walking to Tamassos when Ramon stopped his truck. Though it may have taken him longer, he would still have walked the same road that cuts through the Mesaoria plain and into the small villages surrounding Tamassos. He would have passed the Monastery of Agios Irakleidios and perhaps noticed a canvas bag discarded by its closed gates. He surely would have went over and picked it up, thinking that a passing tourist had mistakenly left it there. He would have untied the string and discovered Bakkar's journals and wondered how they came to be there. Had Bakkar himself been to the monastery that day? But nothing would have changed. He would have carefully studied the engravings on the pillars of the monastery gates and realised the same symbols adorned the journals and the books belonged to the monastery. He was simply blaming everything other than fate for taking him here. Carlos remembered the words of his father.

"When you awaken on a new day, Carlos, before the sun fully rises and heats the land, and your young, glorious eyes open wide, take a deep breath and seize every sense of what is around you into your lungs and your very being, deep into your soul."

8

He sensed the strong rising sun on the closed lids of his eyes. His body stretched out awkwardly and he gripped the iron gates with his hands. He drew in a deep and glorious breath of the most wonderful, fresh morning air. He smelt roses; their sweetness penetrated his lungs. The dew of the morning teased his lips and he arched his stiff back and rolled onto his side. He finally opened his eyes and saw a line of blurred toes. He stumbled up onto his knees.

"Are you okay? Have you been sleeping here all night?"

Carlos still had a firm grip on the bag containing the journals. He looked at the person who had spoken to him on the other side of the gates. It was a young, softly spoken girl and she was not much younger than him. He looked down at her toes again. She had painted them with a silvery-grey varnish that had begun to fade and crack in places.

"Are you a nun?"

"No, but I'm thinking of becoming one. Are you going to stay down there on the ground all morning?"

Carlos felt foolish and he quickly scrambled onto his feet, still clutching the bag. His fingers fidgeted nervously with the end of his shirt. He looked at the girl and she smiled broadly at him. At that moment, he knew her face and he remembered her smile.

"I have something I think might belong to the monastery."

Carlos half-lifted the heavy bag up, but in the morning light he realised its true size and weight.

"Maybe you should come inside and see someone."

"Yes, yes. I'd like that."

Carlos hitched his backpack over his shoulders. The girl unlocked and opened one of the large gates and gestured him to come inside. He stood for a moment, still fixed on the girl's smile. As she led the way through the beautiful monastery gardens, Carlos' heart whispered out a name to him.

Monika...Monika...

"Your name is Monika, isn't it?"

"Yes, it is. How did you know?"

She turned her head quickly around to look at him. She seemed immediately startled.

"I remember you from the market at Lefkosa, Monika. You were a little younger. Well...I mean, you seemed much younger, and we played on the steps of a church and then went inside and you taught me about the Stations of the Cross. You were with your mother and I think I tried to fall in love with you that day."

Carlos was uneasy and embarrassed by the words stumbling foolishly from his lips, but he couldn't hold back the words. They just kept coming, one after the other.

"I suppose I was young and it was the first time I'd been to the market without my father. I was trying very hard to be grown up. Don't you remember me, Monika? I'm Carlos. I was the boy with the bird in the cage on the bus."

Carlos could not believe what he had just said. The girl glared at him, then blushed with a slow and puzzled shake of her head.

"I'm sorry, I don't really remember. I've only been to the Lefkosa market a few times. I don't know why I should remember you anyway."

The words seemed casual and almost cruel to Carlos. He began to doubt his own memory.

Carlos quickly followed the girl up some stone steps. He stood next to her while she pushed open a heavy wooden door. He was sure this girl must be Monika because the voice of his heart told him so.

"What is your name? You're Monika, aren't you?"

"I might be."

She forced a little smile.

"Look, wait here. I'll get someone to speak to you," she said as she disappeared down a dimly lit corridor.

Carlos remembered the young girl he'd played with on the steps of the church in Lefkosa market. She still had the same pretty, round face and speckled nose and petit figure. Her short brown hair had given way to long flowing locks of curls that covered her shoulders and reached right down her back.

Carlos waited in the coolness of a large, old, stone kitchen. He could smell bread freshly baking away in three iron ovens. There were flowers everywhere. He had noticed large pitharia jars outside in the garden filled with flowers of the most amazing colours. Even the kitchen was filled with various sized urns filled with roses of every hue. The huge electric fan spinning above his head delivered a different scent and cooling breeze on each of its slow rotations.

It seemed like he had been waiting an age for her to return. Finally, she appeared in a doorway on the far side of the kitchen. She stood for a moment looking across at him without saying a word. She smiled again and his heart settled into a gentle rhythm. He had not wanted to embarrass her earlier. Her smile had returned and he grew easy in himself. She walked across the kitchen to him and pulled a small stool out from under an oak table.

"Please, sit. The Mother Superior will be here soon. She's in the chapel at the moment."

Carlos sat on the stool and placed his heavy bag at his feet. Monika turned away and began rearranging flowers in a nearby urn. She moved to each urn on the floor in turn, leaning down and carefully fingering the stems and the delicate heads of the roses. Carlos followed her with his eyes around the room. He could hear the swish of her long floral dress as she moved quickly to each one, pausing for just a few moments. She worked her way right around the kitchen giving each urn of flowers the same care and attention. She stopped and finally and looked across at him.

"You were buying hooks, I think—for your father in the market."

"Yes Monika! Hooks and nets...I think."

She smiled broadly again and giggled a little.

"Well, if you don't remember, Carlos..."

When she giggled he knew for sure it was Monika. The memories of that day came flooding back to him. It was as if someone threw a bucket of water over him and he awoke from years of the same pleasant daydream.

"I do remember you, Carlos. I should've said so outside at the gates. But when you got off the bus and I watched you disappear that day on the journey back from Lefkosa, you know I was sure somehow I would see you a day or two later. But it never happened. For a long time, I did miss you. And when I did I just had to think of you and that eagle and how you scowled on the bus. I wanted so much to go with you into the mountains to let the eagle go."

They giggled together for a few moments and then were silent.

"I think it was a long time before I went back to the market. And I never did return to the place where I let the eagle free. I should have gone back, but I didn't."

Carlos hesitated and thought about the day she had spent with him in the church looking at the Stations of the Cross and talking about Christ.

"Why do you want to become a nun? You're so pretty."

"That's a terrible thing to say. You make it sound like every young woman who dedicates herself to Christ is an old ogre. And saying it in a place like this!"

"But I didn't mean it that way; it's just that you're…"

Monika interrupted Carlos.

"I'm Monika. I'm a young woman and I'm happy with that just for now. Let's leave it there."

She smiled again and walked back through the doorway at the far side of the kitchen which led to the main part of the monastery. She left the door ajar and Carlos could make out the flickering of candlelight and the sounds of footsteps on hard stone disappear into the distance.

Monika eventually returned and beckoned him to follow her through the doorway. He picked up the heavy bag and followed her out into what was the main chapel of the monastery. He could see the beautiful ornate, marble altar at the end, and the only source of light came from huge burning candles that lit the far corners of the entire chapel. He was led down a dimly lit corridor past a large study and library. They stopped outside a room with its door ajar.

"Mother Superior..."

Monika knocked on the door gently as she whispered the words. She went to push the door open but paused and turned around to face Carlos behind her.

"I'm so sorry. I do remember so much of that day at the market, but I wouldn't have remembered your name unless you told me. I feel a little ashamed that you remembered mine."

Monika bowed her head, but Carlos could see that she was blushing brightly again.

He whispered gently into her ear.

"I know my name was in your heart and that's all that matters."

"You're so very right, Carlos. And you must tell me what you did with the eagle when you got off the bus."

They tried to stifle their giggles as Monika knocked softly on the door of the room.

"We mustn't keep Mother Superior waiting any longer."

Monika pushed the door open and went inside. Carlos listened to the hushed voices. He could not discern what they were saying but they spoke for a minute or two before Monika came back outside.

"I'll be in the kitchen. Go on inside. Mother Superior will see you now."

She raised her voice much higher on the last few words as she pushed the door open. Carlos stepped inside and heard the door quickly close behind him.

An elderly woman with long, thin, greying hair poking out from under a dark blue habit sat behind an ornate writing table. The light from a window behind her dazzled his eyes. The elderly woman looked up from her desk and removed a pair of wiry framed glasses.

"Now, young man. What can the Sisters of Saint Heracleidius do for you on this glorious morning?"

"I have brought some books for you."

"Books? I don't understand. This is an ecclesiastical monastery for the Sisters of Saint Heracleidius. It's not a bookseller's market, and we don't take donations of books."

Carlos felt the Mother Superior was treating him as if he were a child of the streets. He looked down at his worn clothes and he understood why she might have thought this.

"Please, Mother Superior, I believe these books belong to the monastery."

He hoisted up the heavy bag in front of him.

"Then, young man, you'd better show them to me. Bring them over here."

Carlos walked over to the table and placed the bag on it. The Mother Superior opened the string tied around the neck of the bag and peered inside. She pulled one of Bakkar's journals out and gazed at it, running her long fingers over the embossed insignia on the cover. She flicked through the pages of the journal and then pulled another out of the bag. One by one, she took them out, carefully examining the cover and pages, before placing them one upon the other on her table. She smiled at Carlos when she placed the last of the journals on the top of the pile. Carlos counted them with his eyes. There were eight in all.

"Hmmm. Tell me, how did you come upon these?"

"I bought them...at a market."

Carlos blurted the words out. Since the previous night, he had given little thought to how he would explain why he had the journals. He did not want to speak about Ramon and his sons. He did not want to speak about Bakkar and the goats and his journey back to the Troodos Mountains.

The Mother Superior picked up the top journal again and began to flick slowly through the pages.

"You must be a wealthy young merchant to afford such rare and exquisite journals. And not to mention your ability to spot works of great religious and worldly merit. That or you are a young, unscrupulous vagabond wandering through circles of deceit and sleight of hand. This monastery and the earth it is built upon are alive with the Holy Spirit of Saint Heracleidius who guided the apostles Saint Barnabas and Saint Paul across the Island of Cyprus to bring the word of Christ. His spirit recognises the miracles of life and the goodness in our hearts as well as the need for the exorcism of sin from our souls."

Carlos looked at the Mother Superior and then he bowed his head as if he was in prayer. He could not yet feel the spirit of Saint Heracleidius around him, but he knew he might be able to listen to the words in his heart.

If your hands could reach out across the river what would you grasp, hold firmly, and claim to be yours? You would grasp the sap which seeps from the trees, bathe in it, believing that this would keep you young forever.

You would grasp the leaves of the trees and shake from them their whispers, and know every hidden secret in the world.

You would seize the colour and fragrance from all that lives and grows on the other side of the river and make it yours.

You would grasp the nettles growing by the shore of the river and let them sting you, and in that moment, your heart would awaken in shame and you would know all the pain in the world.

You would look upon the other side of the river and see all that you had taken.

You would see the greyness, dryness and sterility, and in the final moments of your earthly life, you would reach across and return everything you had taken.

"They belonged to my uncle."

"Is your uncle a priest or monk?"

"No, no. He herds goats."

The Mother Superior forced a little smile and then sighed deeply. She rose from the table and walked over to Carlos and put her arm briefly around him.

"You see..."

She stopped and looked at him closely.

"What is your name?"

"It's Carlos. I have been helping my uncle herd his goats for more than a year now. He's had the journals long before I went to live with him."

"This is terribly difficult and I'm still a little curious as to how precisely these journals came into your possession, Carlos. I think it would be better if you spoke to Padre Callico. I'll get someone to fetch him. And perhaps Monika will get you something to eat in the kitchen while you wait."

He followed the Mother Superior back out through the chapel and into the kitchen. Monika was sitting in the kitchen and the Mother Superior spoke quietly to her.

He was worried that the Mother Superior might try and summon the local police. He called to her when she opened the large oak door.

"Mother Superior, will there be trouble for me?"

She smiled, ignored his question, and then nodded briefly at Monika before leaving.

9

Carlos ate some bread with cheese and olives and Monika insisted that he walk with her around the gardens of the monastery. There was not a single area of the monastery grounds not covered with masses of wild flowers and potted plants. Several nuns were already out in the grounds busily tending to their floral paradise. The sun was starting to rise high in the sky and the shade of some olive trees provided Carlos and Monika with a little cover. They sat on some steps at the foot of an incline close to the road outside the monastery. Carlos could hear the exotic sound of birds coming from a very large, wire-canopied cage nearby. Monika explained that the nuns had kept canaries there for many years.

"It's like when we sat on the steps outside the church in the market all those years ago."

Monika did not reply immediately and Carlos grew worried about what she thought of him now.

He smiled curiously at Monika, although she was staring into the distance at the nuns working in the gardens. He thought it amusing that both times they met each other they ended up at religious places. The young woman sitting beside him was in some ways different to the awkward, bare-legged girl who sat on the steps of the church in the Lefkosa market. Her pretty face and dark complexion had not changed at all, but she seemed different, much deeper and more thoughtful now. He noticed she was looking down at her toes and pushing her sandals into the soft sand. It was the first thing he had laid eyes on that morning when she had woken him at the gate.

"Do the nuns not mind you painting them?"

Carlos pointed down at Monika's feet. Monika laughed without actually looking at him directly in the eye. Instead, she looked back across the gardens at the nuns, almost adoringly, as if she were a little child looking up at her parents.

"They love and worship God here, but learnt in the two years I've been here that they equally appreciate the time and devotion they give in the gardens and kitchens. For them it's simply a part of their worship of God and his earthly world. For some of them it's the canaries, for others it's the flowers. And for the rest, maybe the rose-petal

jam and sugar almonds they make in the kitchens."

"Would you like to be a nun?"

Monika continued to watch the nuns. She
seemed in deep thought and Carlos did not know
if she had actually heard him. She stood up from
the steps and walked a few paces towards the
gardens. Carlos stood up to follow her. She
turned around to look at him carefully for the
first time in quite a while.

"When I first came here, all I wanted to do was
become a nun. But the closer I have become to
God, the less sure I am now. Ever since I was
young, I thought it was going to be my destiny.
God means more to me now than just a life of
solitary devotion. I want to share and celebrate
my worship of God, not hide away from the
world."

Carlos was impressed by the passion in Monika's voice and the sense of belief she held deep in
her heart. But the Saint Heracleidius Monastery
was a beautiful place and he could not understand why someone would want to leave such a
place if they did not have to. Though he loved the
freedom of herding and trekking through the
Troodos Mountains and its forests, he thought
the monastery was a beautiful sanctuary for any
soul.

Monika walked back over and sat on the steps again. Carlos did not rejoin her. He pulled uneasily on the ends of his shirt and kicked the loose sand on the ground.

"Your Mother Superior thinks I'm some sort of street vagabond."

"Why? Are you in trouble?"

"I'm not sure. I hope not. Someone called Padre Callico is coming to speak to me. Is that good or bad?"

Monika put her arm on Carlos' shoulder.

"Padre is a very sweet man."

"Then he's nothing to do with the police?"

"Padre has been a part of this monastery since long before the nuns arrived. He has spent most of his life living here. Whatever is going on, Carlos, Padre will understand. You have nothing to worry about."

Carlos wanted to tell Monika everything about the journals, and about Ramon and his sons, and his uncle. He did not want to say anymore until he spoke with Padre Callico. But more than anything else, he did not want Monika to think badly of him. Monika stood up and said she had to return inside to her chores.

"It will be fine, Carlos. Padre Callico should be here soon."

She bent down, kissed him softly on his forehead and walked back to the monastery kitchen.

He sat there and watched the nuns from afar with their small practiced and delicate hands, nurturing the flowering gardens. It was as though they were doing it with their very souls. Their eyes searched the soil for rotting weeds in the brilliance of the sun, as if they were fighting ten thousand evils. Their black and white bodies were as pure as snow and their minds as green as the trees around them. It was as if they were caring for the children they would never have. He thought about his own mother and father. And in that moment, he grew sad, and then angry because the nuns had reminded him of his parents and his loss. He could hear his heart trying to speak, but he would not mouth the words because he feared they would be harsh and unkind words about the nuns and their simple and beautiful existence, hidden away in the monastery. He was ashamed now. He bowed his head down so it almost touched his chest and he read the upside down words printed on his old t-shirt. *Appolonia Nicosia FC*. And then the words of his heart echoed inside him.

Don't be so harsh on others. None of us are without sin.

Carlos stood up to watch one of the nuns open the gates of the monastery. He could see a tall, elderly man dressed in a grey shirt and trousers walking in the gates. He walked with a wooden cane and greeted each gaggle of nuns he passed. Carlos could make out his white collar of devotion as he drew closer. He seemed to have come alone and smiled when he reached Carlos.

"You must be Carlos!"

The old man reached out with his hand even before he was close enough for Carlos to grasp it. The old man gripped his hand firmly and shook it. When Carlos looked into the man's eyes he saw wisdom in an instant. He had a stature and air of authority that reminded Carlos of the wise men of his village.

"But you didn't bring the police with you."

"The police? But why?"

Padre Callico seemed surprised.

"Because of the journals I brought back to the monastery."

Padre Callico bowed his head, shook it gently, and laughed aloud.

"You may be troubled Carlos, but you are not *in trouble.*"

He gestured Carlos towards the monastery door and they began walking together. He noticed Carlos' t-shirt.

"Appolonia Football Club. Not so good for them this year. Dammi...now he's done alright. But Dimitri, he's just come to Cyprus for the climate and the good life, hey!"

"I'm afraid I'm not really much of a football fan, Padre. I've one other t-shirt with Che Guvarra on it, but they just keep me cooler in the midday sun."

They both laughed as they walked through the kitchen and out into the small candlelit church.

Carlos liked Padre Callico. He liked the way his voice boomed one moment and then at times dissipated to almost a whisper. Padre Callico paused for a while in the church and looked around. He took a deep intake of air into his lungs as if he had just stepped outside.

"This is a most beautiful and tranquil place. It's so hard to believe that it has been rebuilt many times over from the ravages of war, bitterness and greed. So many places like this in Cyprus were plundered over hundreds of years."

He whispered these words gently but they still echoed through the church. He sighed deeply and turned to Carlos.

"Are you a godly person, Carlos?"

Carlos was a little surprised by Padre Callico's question, though the more he thought about it, it seemed perfectly in keeping with the sacred place they both stood in.

"I suppose I am, but not because I've searched for God or studied any religious works. If I believe in myself, then I have to believe in God. It's God

MICK ROONEY

who's made me who I am. Does that make sense, Padre?"

"Yes, perfect sense. God is indeed in you and all of us, whatever we believe or think, Carlos."

Padre Callico reached out and embraced Carlos firmly. He whispered something inaudible and Carlos took it to be some kind of blessing.

"Come, Carlos. Let us take a look at these journals you have brought us."

He led Carlos out of the church and down through a narrow passage which led back to the corridor he had been in earlier with the Mother Superior. Padre Callico brought him into a large library room. Several beautiful, ornately polished tables and armchairs furnished the room. Every wall was lined with bookcases that stretched from floor to ceiling. Sunlight flooded in through two large windows on one wall which overlooked the gardens outside. It reminded him of The Palace of Dreams in the mountains next to his village and the many times he'd sneaked away and spent hours hiding there. Padre Callico left him and went to fetch the journals from the Mother Superior's office.

A light breeze began to blow in the open windows and lift the veil curtains on either side of them. Carlos wanted to tell Padre Callico everything he knew about the journals and how Bakkar had written in them every day. He did not

want to get Bakkar into trouble, but he did won-
der how he had come upon them. Carlos sat in a
leather armchair by the window. He could hear
the nuns talking giddily in the garden. They
seemed happy and oblivious to what went on in
the world outside the gates of the monastery. And
though he dreamed of adventures in the Troodos
Mountains, and journeys to the lands farther
east of the island, he felt safe just where he was.

Padre Callico returned carrying the stack of
journals in his hands. He found himself an armchair opposite Carlos by the window. He placed
his cane beside the armchair and laid the journals, one on top of the other, by his feet. He had
no sooner settled in his seat, when he leapt up.

"I'm forgetting my manners, young Carlos...a
drink for both of us!"

Padre Callico walked to a writing table and
poured out two glasses of lemon water with ice
cubes from a large decanter. He handed Carlos
one of the glasses and settled himself back down
in his seat once again.

"Tell me, Carlos. How old are you?"

"Nearly seventeen, Padre. I'm going to travel
back to the Troodos Mountains for a while, and
then, maybe soon, beyond the island, perhaps to
the east...maybe Syria."

"Really, Carlos. Leave beautiful Cyprus. But
what for?"

Carlos was a little surprised by Padre Callico's reply. He thought about his father and his mother, and about the year he had spent with Bakkar in the tower. He thought about the goats on Ramon's farm in Syria and how lazy both his sons probably are. He could picture in his mind working on a farm, helping Ramon and listening to him complain about how his idle sons chasing young girls all day and drinking late into the evenings.

"I've learnt lots of things from my father and my Uncle Bakkar. I can fish and herd goats, haggle with the traders in the markets. I know the trees and rivers of this island like they were part of my own garden."

"They're very useful skills, Carlos. But can you read, can you write about what you have learnt?"

Carlos slumped back in his chair and sipped from his glass. He did not know whether Padre Callico was making fun of his plans or he really thought he was just a simple uneducated boy from a village.

"Padre Callico, there is a place close to the village where I grew up called The Palace of Dreams. The walls are lined with thousands of books. When I was young, very young, I used to run away and hide under the tables with a pile of books from the shelves and leaf through the pages looking at the wonderful pictures for hours on end. My father would summon the elders in the village and say to the other wise men, 'Carlos is gone again, find him.' But the wisest of them knew exactly where I was. And when I returned, they would warn me, 'your father's angry but we will not say where you were.' Finally, my mother found out where I'd been going, and she spoke to my father, and soon he became calm about my visits to The Palace of Dreams. My mother taught me how to read and write, and the elders soon started to help me with my studies. I was the only young boy accepted into The Palace of Dreams. And the memory of what my mother and father did for me will live as long as all the things I learnt in that place—the Incas, the Egyptians, the Romans, and even the memory of the trees that surround the place."

The Padre was silent for a few moments. His head was bowed as if he were deep in thought or praying. Finally, he lifted the glass he held in his lap to his lips and gulped the water down ferociously and quickly. He placed the empty glass by his feet and lifted up one of the journals.

"These are the sacred journals of Saint Heracleidius and they speak of all that has passed in this world since his death. Many hands have toiled under lamplight in this place recording their holy words. They wrote under threat of death and the sound of many battles outside the gates. Some who toiled away on these words died, some lied, and a few left taking the journals they wrote with them. And like them, I have spent many years here, recording my entries."

Padre Callico got up from his seat and turned towards the open window. Carlos followed him with his eyes. He thrust both his hands into his trouser pockets. He seemed unsettled on his legs and after a few moments turned and reached for his cane by the armchair.

"Like you, Carlos, I tended flocks of goats in the mountains. But soon I grew uneasy and realised that God was on my shoulder and I took to looking after a flock of a different kind. It's a flock who can stray a little more easily than the ones I'd grown up with. It took me many years to truly understand them. And yet, sometimes, I still see a few who stray, never to return to God's flock."

Padre Callico turned and sat back down in his chair. He leaned forward and clasped his hands together. Carlos could see that he was holding a holy cross on a band of dark brown beads. He had not noticed them before.

"Let me tell you, Carlos. There is not a thing you will say to me that I'll hate you for. There's no hate in my Father's kingdom. I've lived all my life in his undying gaze. All I hear, he also hears. But only he has the power to judge. It's a relationship of equal dedication and devotion. There are no secrets. And I give you the same pledge that I shared with my *Holy Father*. Let me pledge to you, all that has gone before us in our past will be forgotten and forgiven before we have even fully known each other."

"Yes, Padre."

"Good. Now, tell me how you came upon the journals."

"The journals belonged to Bakkar—my uncle. He kept them in a chest at the bottom of his bed. He wrote in them every evening without fail all the time I lived with him."

"Bakkar..."

Padre Callico said his uncle's name slowly as if he were savouring each syllable.

"Please...go on Carlos."

Carlos told the Padre about Bakkar and the herd of goats and about the farmer Ramon and his sons. He told him about the favour Bakkar had asked of Ramon and the fear he had seen in the eyes of the farmer.

"This is very curious, Carlos. Yet, I'm still puzzled. You see, one of the journals is not complete, and you only have these eight. There should be ten journals in a full volume. It's understood and accepted that all who write in the great journals of Saint Heracleidius must, at the very least, ensure each journal is completed by the same hand. Each scribe of the journals of Saint

Heracleidius is a dedicated scholar and undertakes it with great seriousness."

Carlos could see that the Padre's head was slightly bowed and his brow was lined with trouble. Carlos wanted to tell him everything he knew, but he did not want to speak badly of Bakkar. He did not understand why Bakkar had left so suddenly, and why he sold the herd and left the journals in the hands of a simple farmer from Syria. He must have known their importance and that their destiny lay with the monastery of Saint Heracleidius. Carlos knew Padre Callico was being good to him and he wanted to be true to the Padre.

"Padre Callico. You're right. There are two other journals. I have them in my backpack. But they're blank. My uncle gave them to me, but I don't exactly understand why."

The Padre lifted his head when Carlos spoke. His brow was no longer lined and heavy. He smiled at Carlos and stood up. He gripped Carlos' shoulders firmly.

"I think I understand, Carlos. But you must trust me first."

Padre Callico paced the library for a few moments. Carlos listened to the tapping of his cane on the marble floor. Padre Callico walked around the room gripping his nose between his index finger and thumb and sighed deeply. Carlos did not want to say anything. He did not want to interrupt the Padre's train of thought. The Padre finally returned to his seat and began to feverishly tap his finger against his lips.

"Carlos. I knew your uncle. He spent many years of religious study and silent devotion here at Saint Heracleidius. That he took the journals from here is nothing. He did this many times when he travelled on missions to Africa and the Middle East."

Padre Callico turned and looked out the window. He seemed distracted for a second.

"Come, Carlos. I want to show you some things."

Padre Callico leapt up from his seat quickly and for a moment he seemed unsteady on his feet and Carlos reached out to grasp him.

"I'm fine, I'm fine! Come with me."

The Padre shrugged off Carlos' attention and walked towards the door. Carlos followed him out, down the corridor, and into the Mother Superior's office. Padre Callico pointed to a large framed photograph on the wall. Carlos peered up at it. It was a group of monks dressed in brown cloaks. Carlos recognised the gardens and part of the monastery in the background.

"The man in the centre is Bakkar, your uncle. And to his right is a very much younger Padre Callico."

The Padre laughed a little and led Carlos back towards the kitchen.

"The cloaks must have been uncomfortable to wear in the heat, Padre?"

"Oh, it was just for the photograph. We sometimes wore flip-flops and shorts. It was all about the work we did, Carlos, not how we looked. Now, let's walk in the gardens for a while. The sun will be at its warmest in an hour or two, and then it will be time for me to lie down for a while. We must decide what it is we both have to do."

They walked outside into the gardens. Carlos could see Monika. She was helping the nuns. He paused for a moment letting Padre Callico walk a few steps in front of him. The Padre noticed Carlos looking across at the nuns working away in the gardens.

"I take it the beautiful gardens of Saint Heracleidius are not the only thing to capture your heart, hmmm?"

"Sorry, Padre."

Carlos blushed a little.

"Not at all. She is a delightful young girl with spirit and dedication. She's been working here for a while, but I'm not so sure about her strength of belief and calling. With dedication, sometimes there comes a great personal sacrifice. Though the hand of God will guide us, he can't pull our

spirit through life if it becomes heavy with distraction and delusion."

"You mean sin, Padre?"

"Not so much sin, Carlos. Sin is the material
manifestation of man's mortal journey through
life. As a man of God's work, I actually expect it. I
don't see it as my divine purpose to condemn it.
Sin is not rational; it's just another excuse to ig-
nore the truth your heart speaks."

They strolled for a little while and neither of
them spoke a word. Padre Callico walked quite
slowly and habitually tapped his cane on the
winding gravel path. He was tall and thin and
walked bolt upright. Occasionally, he would
whistle and sing a song about a blackbird. Carlos
wondered what the Padre would advise him to do.
Only yesterday, he had wanted to lose himself in
the Troodos Mountains, but now he realised this
was perhaps the distraction and delusion Padre
Callico spoke of. He did not want his spirit to be
weighed down by all that had happened. The
journals were Bakkar's. He had entrusted them
to a farmer in the market in the hope that they
would return safely to the monastery. He could
not understand why Bakkar gave up the herd of
goats to Ramon, and for nothing other than the
promise of the journals being safely returned.
Had Ramon not stopped his truck last night for

Carlos, the journals could have ended up any-where.

"Carlos, it's time for me to rest a while."

Padre Callico seemed a little out of breath. He slumped down on a small wall under some olive trees. He leaned forward and mopped his brow with a large cloth handkerchief he pulled from his trouser pocket. He doubled the handkerchief over and draped it over his head.

'Padre. Are you okay?"

"I'm fine, Carlos. The heat just gets to me more than it used to."

The Padre rested his arms on his knees and then slid the handkerchief down over his face. He wiped his face thoroughly and then returned it to his trouser pocket.

"Are you sure you don't want to return in-doors, Padre?"

"Please, Carlos. I'm fine. It's foolish. Now, what are we to do?"

Right then, bells sounded out from the monas-tery tower. The Padre stood up with the help of his cane and fidgeted from pocket to pocket of his trousers.

"It's noon, Carlos. A moment..."

He eventually pulled out a small bottle of tab-lets from his pocket and tossed two of them into his mouth. He sat back down and breathed in and out deeply, stifling a cough with his hand.

"Excuse me, Carlos. The air dries my throat."

Padre Callico began whistling and singing about the blackbird again. He tapped his cane to the beat as he sung. He seemed uneasy and nervous to Carlos.

"Padre, we can talk later if you want."

"No. We talk now. Carlos, are you a child of God? Have your parents brought you up in the light of God?"

"My parents are both dead. Although I'm not a child who spent much time in churches. I have been brought up in the words of God. And the words were as present and real as the trees that greeted us outside our home every morning."

"Then you're probably more a child of God than many consider themselves."

"But Padre, I cursed God and all that happened when I lost my parents."

"Shh...Say nothing more. The Great Father hears all you say and also the words your heart speaks."

Carlos tried at that moment to listen to his heart. He closed his eyes and he saw his parents together. They were happy and he could hear Padre Callico whistling again and the tapping of his cane on the gravel. He could see the blackbird and it was no longer the young blackbird in Padre's song. It was strong and it soared high up into the heavens. And below, as if Carlos rode upon its back, he could see the Troodos Mountains and the coastline of all of Cyprus. He could see Ramon and his sons loading the herd of goats onto a large boat at Limassol. At that moment, he let go of the blackbird. He did not want to weigh it down any farther on its journey beyond the island. He knew the blackbird was free.

"He came to me one day, out of the blue, and said he was leaving."

Carlos looked at Padre Callico. He, in turn, was looking directly at him.

"Your uncle...you see we studied for many years together here in Saint Heracleidius. The convent wasn't here back then. It was just the twelve of us, each highly knowledgeable in a particular field of learning; from religious theology, Greek philosophy to languages. There seemed nothing we didn't know. And with this knowledge we recorded the history of mankind in the journals since the birth of Our Lord. But that was just the start because we vowed to record not just what mankind had done, but all that would happen in the future. By looking deeply into the past you can learn so much about the future. But while we write under the power and light of God's hand, we are ultimately mortal beings, of flesh and blood. As dedicated as we all were, we grew tired and older. Like Bakkar, they all eventually left to spread their knowledge across the world.

Some have since died through the afflictions of disease and war, and some of the others, like Bakkar, toil away at their journals. Once every so often, a journal will arrive from Africa, Australia, or South America. I place them with the rest of the collection in the library. I believe all the journals will return one day, but perhaps not in my lifetime."

Carlos was fascinated by the thought that once in the great library of the monastery these twelve men had laboured over their journals, their heads filled with ancient civilizations and battles. He imagined it the same way he remembered The Palace of Dreams. He would have given anything to know what Bakkar had undertaken during the evenings he watched him scribble away in his journals.

"Padre, why did my uncle leave the monastery so suddenly?"

"He left to walk the road to Damascus and trace the footsteps of Saint Paul. He'd been studying the life of Saint Paul for many months. You see, it was Saint Paul and Saint Barnabas who brought Christianity to Cyprus in the first century. When they arrived in Cyprus they met Saint Heracleidius and declared his home, which was a small cave not far from here, to be the first Christian church. He became the first bishop of Tamassos and he built this monastery. The road to Damascus has great religious significance. Saint Paul set out from Jerusalem to travel to Damascus to destroy Christianity but Christ appeared to him along the road and so the course of Saint Paul's life changed. He reached Damascus and was baptised. He spent the rest of his life spreading the word of Christ. I believe Bakkar reached a point of spiritual doubt, questioning why he was doing what he was doing. He left the monastery hours after sharing his spiritual distractions with me. He took ten journals with him and I've never laid eyes on him since."

The Bakkar that Padre Callico talked of seemed quite different to the one Carlos had grown to know. Though Carlos knew Bakkar had remained a spiritual man, he also knew that Bakkar had grown himself a harsh exterior. If what the Padre said was true about Bakkar travelling on the road to Damascus all those years ago, then perhaps Christ had not really appeared to his uncle like Saint Paul. And perhaps he had returned to the island more troubled and disillusioned with his own beliefs.

"I don't think my uncle saw Christ when he travelled to Damascus, Padre. He doesn't seem like a man who has met Christ."

"Maybe he didn't. There are thousands of people the world over who travel great distances to walk pilgrimages and pray at the holiest altars of

Our Lord. Lourdes, Jerusalem, Rome, and though in their hearts they may want to see Christ or Mother Mary, they return home undefeated, and the power of God still remains strong in their spirit. Some of these pilgrims are troubled, weak, even dying, but they actually realise they already had the strength of light in their spirit which appeared to Saint Paul on the road to Damascus. The purpose of the journey and the pilgrimage is to turn belief into realisation. When Saint Paul reached Damascus and told the people of Christ appearing to him, perhaps he lied. He may have walked that long journey from Jerusalem and grew deeply remorseful in his heart about his treatment of the Christians. And into the arms of Anaden he threw himself to be baptised under the gaze of Christ. What's clear is that self forgiveness is equally as important as forgiveness from those we sin against. Saint Paul left Damascus with Christ deep in his heart. But did your uncle leave Damascus full of self forgiveness?"

Carlos thought for a while about what the Padre had said. He thought about Bakkar. If he could find him and bring him to the monastery, then he could hear what Padre Callico had to say. He could help Bakkar finish the journals. He could work for a time in the markets and save some money to buy more goats.

"Padre. I should find my uncle and bring him here. I owe it to him. He took me in when I left my village."

"Carlos. Your uncle is on his journey and you mustn't assume that your paths are linked. I'm sure your uncle was there for you when it was necessary. That is what family is for. You may spend the rest of your life looking for your uncle and never find him. If I know your uncle well enough, then I don't believe you will find him. He does not wish to be found. But if you wish to make a young man's journey a life-long folly, then so be it. Finish writing the two journals he has given you. Write whatever you wish. And of the eight that you have returned to us—just one remains unfinished. It will remain here, and if your uncle doesn't return to claim and finish it, then you must return to finish it one day. This is the way it should be."

Carlos felt a great weight of decision upon him. He could see that Padre Callico had grown tired. He watched him take the handkerchief and mop his brow again. He stood up and steadied himself with his cane.

"I think it's time I had that nap of mine. I've promised the Mother Superior I'd help her with this evening's service. We can speak afterwards. I'll speak to her about getting you a bed for however long you need. Rest easy, Carlos. Stay and appreciate God's beauty for a while."

Carlos watched Padre Callico walk slowly back towards the monastery doorway. The Padre emerged back outside a few minutes later and walked down towards the gate. He stopped briefly to speak with the nuns but was soon on his way. Carlos closed his eyes and he could feel the sun shining directly onto his face. He could hear the insects fly close by, browsing amongst the fruits of the olive trees above, but they did not bother him. Through a window not far away, he thought he could smell freshly baked bread. His nose twitched and he brushed an insect away with his hand. He was still thinking of the blackbird. He sensed someone moving close by and opened his eyes. For a moment, the rays of the sun dazzled him and he had to shield his face with his hand. Then he saw Monika standing above him.

"We're baking bread for this evening's service. Did things go okay with the Padre?"

Monika sat down beside him, but she did not wait for him to answer her.

"The Padre is a very special man. He's wise and does so much for us here."

Monika gushed with enthusiasm as if she were talking fondly about a beloved grandparent.

"I don't think the Padre is very well, Monika."

Monika did not say anything for a moment. Instead, she rubbed her shins up and down with her hands and rested her chin on her knees.

"I've heard the nuns talking about him, Carlos. He's dying. They say he has cancer. It's in his legs and he may not be able to walk much longer."

"I think it's very sad, Monika. He's so undeserving of that."

Monika stood up and beckoned Carlos to follow her back inside. But Carlos remained where he was.

"Did the Padre say he would help you?"

"Yes, yes he did. He used to know my uncle. They both studied together here many years ago before the nuns took over the monastery. He said he would speak with the Mother Superior and I could stay here tonight. But I'm not so sure."

"Carlos, you must!"

Monika quickly sat back down beside Carlos and put her arm round him. She smelt of olives and fresh bread. He could see small dust flecks of flour on her printed summer dress.

"You will be safe here until you decide what you've to do."

Right then, Carlos was unsure what he should do. He did not want to leave Monika. He wanted to spend more time with Monika in the monastery, but his heart spoke about a journey, and all hearts must undertake a journey that can become difficult and painful. Carlos did not know whether he was ready or not. A part of him longed for the isolation and beauty of the Troodos Mountains, and not the road Saint Paul had taken to Damascus. He felt he was unafraid. But he knew the journey was his own and he would walk alone.

He thought about Ramos, the farmer from Syria, about Bakkar on his own journey, about Padre Callico dying from the disease inside him and his quest for the all the completed journals. He thought about Monika and whether she would become a nun in the monastery, and then he became anxious and afraid. The thoughts consumed him. He sensed Monika's uneasiness. She stood up without saying another word and walked back to the monastery.

10

The Mother Superior showed him to a small room at the back of the monastery. It had a wardrobe, a bed, and a small wooden locker with an electric lamp on it. When she left, he stretched his body out on the bed and gazed at the ceiling. After a while he could hear the footsteps of the nuns outside his door.

He slept for a few hours and dreamed about the many journeys ahead. He could hear the voice of Tass reading aloud to him and he knew the words were from the journals. It would soon be time for him to create his own words in the journals and begin his next journey.

It is time Carlos. It is time.

He awoke and sat up in his bed. The whole monastery was filled with the sound of the nuns singing from the church. He knew Padre Callico was celebrating mass that evening. He got up and crept out into the semi-darkness of the corridor. The nuns had stopped singing and he could hear the voice of Padre Callico. He stood outside the doorway of the church and listened.

"There are few sins we cannot seek the act of contrition for. The apostle Paul left Jerusalem, and in his heart he wanted to end the power of Christianity and its spread throughout the world. He scorned and derided the very word and fruits of the man who proclaimed it to others. He saw the great city of Damascus as the citadel of Christianity and he chose to bring about its downfall. Saint Paul was one man against a belief and a city. It must have taken him great courage to believe he could do this. Saint Paul believed he could. And on each step of the road to Damascus, he must have grown stronger in his belief. A man's belief sometimes becomes the dominion which entraps his very spirit.

"We must seek on our life's journey to enrich our spirit and grow evermore knowledgeable, and to enlighten all those around us. Each step forward must invigorate us. We must believe what we do is right. And, when Saint Paul travelled forward on the road to Damascus, his journey, through every step, must have become filled with questions and doubt. How could he challenge the power of Christ? And upon this road, no believer in Christ dared to stop or challenge him. He must have thought to himself that the power of Christ was waning. Saint Paul was on his journey and the people of Damascus did not know their belief in Christ was to be challenged. When you are on your journey of discovery, you don't travel with an army. Those who travel on a journey with an army seek only to impose their will by force, oppression and terror. Their purpose is to take land and overpower political and religious balance. Saint Paul travelled alone on his journey. Only one true friend showed himself along the way and this was the light and presence of Jesus Christ himself, whom he had already forsaken. And the light and presence of Jesus Christ filled his very soul.

"We sometimes grow lonely on our journey. We look for strength, guidance and enlightenment, which tells us we are on the right course. We look ahead on the road for signs of reassurance, but in our hearts, we know why we are there. When Saint Paul arrived in the city of Damascus, he was bathed in the light and waters of baptism and the power of Our Lord. He chose, thereafter, to bring this light to the beautiful island of Cyprus. Let us pray, like Saint Paul we will meet and be guided on our paths by the hand of Christ, and we too may be moved upon our journey."

After the service the nuns left the church and the place became quiet. Carlos sat for a while in the kitchen of the monastery. Padre Callico appeared in the doorway. He smiled at Carlos.

"Are you comfortable there?"

"Yes, Padre. I liked your sermon and what you said about Saint Paul."

"You were there?"

"I listened outside the door."

"But Carlos, you should have come inside. You were more than welcome."

"I know, Padre."

"Are you ready for your journey, Carlos?"

"Yes, Padre. I am."

"Then we will speak again in the morning."

Padre Callico walked over and blessed Carlos before leaving. Carlos sat in the kitchen a while longer He could still smell the bread that had been baked earlier that day. The kitchen was cool and his eyes grew heavy with tiredness. He took a glass of water with him to bed. His thoughts were peaceful and soon he was fast asleep.

Monika came into his room late that night. He had heard the door creek but had not stirred. He knew he could come to no harm in the monastery. Though it was dark, he knew it was Monika. He could smell the bread and the olives from her skin. He could hear her take off her nightgown and then felt her slip into the bed bedside him.

He only stirred when she placed her hands on his shoulder. She whispered to him.

"Carlos, do you want to make love to me?"

He froze and he felt his heart beat quickly. He did not know how. He turned in the bed to face her in the darkness. He held her close to him because he was afraid that she would leave.

"I'm not sure I know how, Monika."

She hugged him closely and rested her head on his chest. They talked for a little while about swimming in the nearby lake and how the fish danced on the surface of the water. Soon, they were both fast asleep *together*.

They awoke to the brightness of the morning. Carlos could hear a wood pigeon outside the window. He knew it was still quite early. Monika stirred and pulled away from his arms. She sat up suddenly, realising where she was. She sat for a few moments on the side of the bed.

"I should go back to my room."

"Why?"

"Oh, Carlos. I'm sorry! I shouldn't have come here last night."

"So you wish you hadn't?"

"No, of course not, Carlos. It was sweet and wonderful to hold you close all night."

He watched her put on her nightgown. She sat back down on the bed placing her hands on her bare knees. It reminded him of the time they both sat on the steps of the church together in the market square. Carlos sat up in bed and put his arm around Monika.

She turned around and looked at him intently.

"Padre Callico gave a nice sermon last night. I wish you could have heard it, Carlos. I just know he was thinking of you when he spoke those words about Saint Paul."

"I did hear it. I was listening outside."

"Then you won't be staying here for a while?"

"No. I can't, Monika."

"Will I see you again?"

"Oh, Monika!"

Carlos put both his arms around her. Her body seemed stiff and unyielding to his gesture.

"There's a part of me that wants you to leave here and come with me. I don't want you to be-come a nun."

"Carlos. That's not a nice thing to say."

"But it's true."

Carlos was sombre and he took his arms from around Monika and began to dress himself. When he was dressed, he walked to the small window and looked out on the gardens of the monastery,

"You're just sulking, and anyway, maybe I don't want to become a nun."

"Then don't."

"I won't!"

Monika got up from the bed and slammed the door of the room when she left.

Monika was at the stove when he went to the kitchen. Carlos could hear Padre Callico outside talking with some of the nuns. His voice boomed out and Carlos sensed the Padre was in a very jovial mood. The door of the kitchen swung open and he stepped in waving his cane in front of him.

"It's a beautiful day, my children, and this afternoon I'll be going to the football final and then I'm going to enjoy some Chilean wine under the moonlight, but only if my team wins!"

Padre Callico pulled a stool from under the table and sat down. He sat close to Carlos, playfully nudging him with his shoulder. He placed his cane on the table and clapped his hands together.

"Monika, bring some cool tea and join us."

"But Padre, I need to..."

"No, no. Not today. It's Sunday. You young ones are coming with me to the football and then we'll gaze at the stars when it gets dark. We'll drink a little wine and Carlos will tell us about his journey and his plans, and you, Monika, will tell us about yours."

They left the monastery early that afternoon and travelled to Lefkosa with Padre Callico in his small car. He sang the blackbird song all the way there and, again, all the way back to his small villa close to the monastery. He filled them all day with cola and hotdogs and his passion for football. His spirits in the evening were still quite high even though his team had only managed a draw in the match, and a replay the following weekend. They sat together outside on a large wooden deck at the back of his villa. The evening was cool and pleasant and darkness drew slowly across the clear sky above them. He passed them small glasses of wine and leaned back in his wicker chair and released a deep sigh of contentment.

Carlos watched Padre Callico's eyes scan the black canopy above them. It was as if he was looking for something very specific, like a keepsake casually placed to one side, and he was only now remembering it. Carlos could hear the sound of goat bells nearby. He looked out into the darkness across the countryside. He could not make out anything through the gloom, though he could hear the whispering of the trees around him. The goats must have heard the whispering trees as well. The herd, wherever they were sheltering in the shadows of the countryside, seemed unsettled. Carlos started to think about Bakkar. He wondered if Bakkar could see and hear the same things somewhere else on the island at that very moment. He looked across at Monika. She had been very quiet all day and had hardly said a word in the car on the way back. He wondered if she was thinking about the night before. She had laughed just once that day when Padre Callico had dropped his cola while celebrating his team's equalising goal. His cup had fallen on his trousers when he leapt from his seat in the stadium to celebrate.

"No, no. I look like I've peed myself!"

Carlos laughed a little to himself when he thought about what Padre Callico had said. Monika did not notice his laughter and the Padre was still too busy looking for whatever he had mislaid amongst the stars above. Carlos wanted to tell the Padre that he knew he was dying, and that he understood death and the loss of something very precious. He felt his eyes water a little and he wiped them on his sleeve. He felt silly, and though the wine was probably making his mind fuzzy and his mood melancholic, he was sure of one thing. The Padre did not care anymore, at least not about himself. He had already fulfilled his own journey.

"We should go, Carlos. Let the Padre rest."

Monika stood up and placed her full glass of wine on the small table beside them.

"No, please. I want both of you to stay a little while longer. I like the company of young minds. Why spoil the serenity, hey, Monika?"

Monika reluctantly sat back down in her chair.

Padre Callico was silent for a few minutes before he pulled his chair properly around to face his two companions. He refilled his large wine glass from the jug on the table.

"You know, I wanted to be a footballer when I was your age. I knew my life should be filled with passion, a physical as well as spiritual passion, and not just with all the books of political and theological knowledge I was studying. We played football not far from here. And in the evenings I would do my theology studies, always falling asleep with a book in my hand, and dreaming of Eusabio and Pelé, the sweet magicians of the football fields. It's silly really, but so true."

Padre Callico reached forward from his chair and sipped from his glass of wine.

"Do you both dream of what you will be one day?"

He looked at both of them in silence. Monika sat forward in her chair. She seemed alerted by Padre Callico's question, as if she had been waiting all day for it to be asked.

"Yes, Monika. Go on. Tell me what's in your heart. Can you tell me what it is you dream of?"

"Papa and Mama always wanted me to be a nun. Both of them sheltered me a lot when I was young. But you must understand, Padre, it was their dream, not mine. When I was a young girl with my dolls, I always wanted to be a nurse. I still do. I want to heal suffering, but not always through the path of Christ. But I'm so afraid of letting Papa and Mama down."

"Ah, I see, Monika, but at the expense of letting yourself down? You must listen to what's in your heart. You mustn't deny the path that's right for you. The power of God's work will be done through your hands and your thoughts, so long as you are true to yourself."

"But Padre, I feel I'm letting you and my parents down. You've been so good to me."

"Then you must be courageous and let us down, not yourself. You cannot let yourself become a vessel for all our regrets and failings."

Padre Callico refilled his glass and offered the rest to Carlos.

"And what did your parents want of you, Carlos?"

Carlos was thinking about his own journey and the choices he should make. He did not take the wine from Padre. He was also thinking about what Monika had just said. He felt Monika would make a wonderful nurse. Her eyes were bright and sincere and he knew she cared so much about the people around her, perhaps too much.

The wind had picked up a little and the trees nearby were chattering away again. He looked across at them and tried to listen to their words. But they all seemed lost to him. He knew they were talking about him, teasing him with their secrets of the past and future. His heart raced a little. He wanted to get up from his chair and run blindly into the darkness of the night. He could not understand why the trees were taunting him. He stood up and walked to the edge of the deck. For the first time in a while, he sensed Tass close by. It was the voice that had first spoken to him on a lonely roadside when he left his village.

"Carlos. Are you okay?"

Carlos could hear Padre, but he did not answer him. He was listening to the trees and his eyes searched the darkness as if he might catch sight of Tass for the very first time.

"Carlos, Carlos!"

He felt Padre Callico's hand grip his arm. It was a little cold. He turned to see Padre standing next to him.

"Please, Carlos. Come and sit back down with us."

Carlos sat back down in his chair, but his eyes fixed again on the darkness.

"I'm sorry, Padre. I thought I heard someone."

"It's nothing, Carlos, just the wind."

Carlos wanted Tass to say something. But there was silence.

"What is it, Carlos? What's troubling you?"

"The trees are mocking me and I don't know why. I don't know what I should do."

"What do you want to do, Carlos?"

"I'm worried about Bakkar, my uncle. And I don't know why I've ended up with the burden of these journals. I want to walk the same road he walked, like Saint Paul in your sermon."

"Why? Because you might find Bakkar there?"

Carlos stared at Padre Callico. He sensed the harshness of his words.

"No man walks the road of revelation a second time. If he dares, then he is blind as well as being a fool. You won't find your uncle on the road to Damascus. Though, I agree, perhaps you may find something more worthy. Only you will know: But, I warn you, Carlos, you may return disillusioned and saddled with a very heavy heart. What you find there, or don't find, may haunt your spirit and thoughts for the rest of your life."

He walked the short journey back to the monastery with Monika. They were silent for most of the journey until they reached the gates. Carlos looked up at the clear sky above them as she opened the heavy gate.

"Come on, Carlos. It's late. What are you looking at?"

"It's the only thing that never seems to change."

Carlos was thinking about the many shepherds who watched over their flocks in the mountains each night. They slept under the same sky for thousands of years and never questioned it being there. He followed Monika inside the gate. The wind blew a little harder and he could hear the trees still whispering around him. Monika walked a few paces ahead of him towards the door of the monastery. Without warning, he heard Tass speak to him.

You must walk the same path many others have walked. It is a path walked by kings and paupers and saints and sinners alike, but all have walked upon this path with equal steps. You may choose to walk heavily with purpose and conviction in your stride, or you may choose to walk lightly with fear and shame in your heart. But, nonetheless, you must walk. You may find nothing but the stones and sand under the soles of your feet and return as you were. You may look deeply at the stones and sand and they may reveal their secrets to you. What you bring on your journey is no more than you will return with.

"Carlos! Please, come inside."

They sat for a while in the kitchen under candlelight. Carlos kept thinking about what he had heard Tass say to him. He did not want to walk the road to Damascus empty-handed. He vowed he would take the two journals with him. It seemed right.

"What are we going to do, Carlos?"

Carlos looked at Monika. He could see from her face that she was tired. She smiled at him and reached across the table to touch his hand. He gripped it tightly.

"You are going to become a wonderful nurse."

She smiled, and for the first time that day, Carlos knew Monika was happy.

"And what's Carlos going to do?"

"I think Padre Callico wants me to become the next Pelé!"

They giggled and Monika let go of his hand.

"Carlos. What will you really do?"

"I'm going to Syria in the morning to walk the road to Damascus."

He could see the surprise in Monika's face.

"Well, I suppose it does sound very daring and exciting, Carlos."

"Then, will..."

Carlos was about to ask Monika to come with him. Something deep inside stopped him immediately. He felt Monika was envious of him. Tomorrow, she would have to face her parents and tell them she did not want to be a nun and, instead, study and become a nurse. He wondered if his own mother and father were alive now, what they would think of his wish to walk the road to Damascus.

The morning breeze surrounded both of them as they stood together in the gardens of the monastery. Carlos had spent the last half an hour preparing a little food and provisions to take with him on his journey. Monika kissed him quickly on the lips. He could taste the olives. It was sudden and he had not expected it. Within moments, she fled inside with just a whisper of goodbye in his ear. He could hear her talking to the nuns in the kitchen of the monastery. The door was still ajar. He could tell Monika was upset. Her eyes had been puffy and red since she rose from his bed that morning. Now, he could hear the nuns inside laughing with her. They were teasing her, joyfully. He turned and walked to the gates of the monastery. Padre Callico beeped the horn of his car again. It must have been the fourth or fifth time he'd sounded it. He finally stopped when he saw Carlos at the gates.

Carlos got into the car and placed his backpack by his feet.

"I hope you have everything you'll need."

"I haven't forgotten the two journals if that's what you mean, Padre."

Padre Callico sighed. He pulled away from the monastery and did not say a word for most of the journey until the coast came into view. Padre Callico had asked him earlier in the morning if he was sure he wanted to travel to Syria. Carlos had nodded in agreement and a roll of money held together with an elastic band was placed into his hand.

"I don't know how far it will take you, but I need to know that you'll be safe. Take it. You must do the rest."

Carlos sat in the car and looked at the boats moored along the coast of Limassol. Only two nights before, Ramon and his sons would have boarded the ferry to return home to their farm in Syria.

"Do you know you will be travelling across the blessed lands of Christ when you reach Israel?"

Carlos had not thought much about the actual road he would take to Damascus. He knew about the biblical Holy lands of the Middle East and that Damascus was one of the oldest inhabited cities in the world.

"I hadn't really thought about it, Padre."

"You see, Saint Paul travelled north from Jerusalem in Israel to Damascus in southern Syria.

The lands you will travel through are hallowed, but treacherous places."

Padre Callico sighed again.

"Are you really sure about this, Carlos?"

"I'm sure, Padre."

He fixed Carlos with a deep stare, and the boy could see Padre's face was pale and tired. The horn of the ferry sounded and broke a brief silence between them. Carlos could see cars and people starting to board the ship. He was leaving his little island home for the first time. He had read books about many far off and exotic places in The Palace of Dreams throughout his childhood. In his mind, he had dreamed and travelled to many of those places, but he could not fool his heart. He was leaving Cyprus...leaving his home.

11

When the ferry slowly moved out of the port of Limassol for Tel Aviv, Carlos rushed up to the top deck of the ship. He could see Padre Callico standing beside his little blue car. He was smoking a cigarette and leaning with both elbows on the roof. Carlos waved limply at him. Padre seemed in a world of his own. He watched Padre for as long as he could see him from the ship. He could see the blue car leaving the port and winding along the coastal road. Soon, it faded away into the protection of the countryside.

The deck of the ship thronged with the bustle and chatter of strange accents and languages. It reminded him of the market at Lefkosa. He could see his island home growing smaller as the ship reached the open sea. It was as if it were slowly sinking into the water. He thought about the lost continent of Atlantis and how it had been engulfed in a great flood. He walked from the rear of the ship to the front deck. His back was to his homeland and his eyes were fixed in the distance on the horizon of the sea. Although the sky was clear, there was a mist in the distance and he could not see any sign of land ahead.

When Padre Callico had first arrived at the monastery that morning, he sat in the kitchen with Carlos and spoke of the journey to Damascus.

"It's a long and arduous journey, Carlos. It's a pilgrimage of the soul as well as the land. You cannot take such a journey lightly. You must be a warrior of your beliefs, whatever they are. To waver, to err, will lead you into the hands of the deceivers, the tricksters and the highwaymen. The light of the sun will guide you on your way, but it may also sap the very energy keeping you awake. The darkness of the night will help keep you hidden from those who wish to do you harm, but you may also stumble helplessly like a blind man. Use every gift you are blessed with and believe in yourself and your instincts, and trade nothing on the road to Damascus. If you are truly to make this journey as a man, then you must walk every footstep tread by Bakkar, as well as Saint Paul and all the pilgrims who have followed him, never once veering from the path of your destiny. And if you do that, you may still return disillusioned, bitter and defeated."

Padre Callico had not been as warm and re-laxed as he had been the previous night at his villa. He had appeared tense and agitated all morning. Carlos wondered if he had not expected him to go through with his journey. He thought more about Padre's words. Did Padre believe Bakkar failed on his journey to Damascus? Padre had talked about his uncle returning to Cyprus disillusioned. Carlos felt an even greater weight on his shoulders. He had wanted to walk the road to Damascus for his mother and father. He wanted to show them who he had become. He wanted to know why Bakkar had given up on life and he vowed it would not happen to him. He wanted to walk the road to Damascus, like Saint Paul, because he believed he could not go on with his life if he did not. It seemed the only way, and for once it felt right.

He found a seat below deck and dozed for a while. It was difficult to sleep because the boat was packed with people. Some sat and rested on the floor in the aisles. Children, bored and rest-less, scampered in and out of the seats and ran up and down the ship after each other. He tried to think about Monika. She would have to tell her parents about wanting to leave the monastery to become a nurse. He wondered if she would stay true to herself.

He slept for some time and was finally roused by a heavy jolt to his shoulder. A man passed by pulling a trolley with three large suitcases piled precariously, one on top of the other. Most people around him were standing up and slowly funneling towards the exits at either end of the ship. He grabbed his knapsack and tried to push his way through the throng of people. Some glared at him, while others simply stood their ground. He gave up and waited for the queue to wind its way off the boat. He could not see very much out of the porthole windows. He might as well have been anywhere.

"When are you returning to Cyprus?"

A man sat perched on a high wooden stool behind a stall. The people ahead of Carlos pushed their documents away into their luggage and moved on.

"So, how long?"

"A week...maybe ten days."

"Where's your return ferry ticket?"

Carlos handed his ticket to the clerk. He spent a minute or two shuffling Carlos' paperwork around his desk. Finally, he pounded his stamp across the paperwork several times and handed the sheets back in a messy pile to Carlos.

"Then I will see you again in ten days, yes?"

"Yes...of course."

Carlos hoped he could make the journey to Damascus in that time. He could always return by train or bus to Tel Aviv. He walked along the coastline for a while drinking from a bottle of water he had bought. The place reminded him of Cyprus. The sandy beaches were filled with tourists basking in the mid-afternoon sunshine. The sky above seemed to continually rumble with the sound of aircraft taking off and landing at a nearby airport.

He was puzzled by some of the strangely shaped buildings that spilled out along the beaches. One rose up high into the air like a huge, circular, battlement tower. He finished his water and placed the bottle in a litter bin with a swarm of wasps hovering over it. He crossed over the bustling street and tried to find the bus station. He knew he needed to reach Jerusalem before nightfall. He would have many tiring and difficult days ahead, and good food and a long rest would prepare him well for tomorrow.

Carlos did not have to look hard to find the central bus station in the city. He almost stumbled upon it while he looked for a place that sold maps. Jerusalem was a lot closer than he had imagined. The driver of the bus assured him they would be there in forty-five minutes. He unfolded the map he had bought and traced his finger along the contours and folds until his fingertip reached Jerusalem. He knew it was an ancient and sacred realm. When the bus drew closer to the city, Carlos could see a myriad of spires, towers and domes stretching far across the skyline. The ornate buildings reminded him of the many churches and monasteries dotted across the mountains and countryside of Cyprus. It seemed every other building in Jerusalem was a place of spiritual adoration and worship.

He wondered where he should get off the bus in this fabulous city. The bus had already begun to empty. People gathered up their bags and belongings and slowly filed off, one after the other, to the comfort and safety of beautiful and luxurious hotels. Each time the bus stopped at one of these great palaces, he read the names adorning their doorways. Some of the places had names that sounded like kings and queens resided there: *The King David, American Colony,* and *Mount Zion.* Carlos knew he could not afford to stay in these places. He put his map away in his backpack and moved to an empty seat at the front of the bus. When the bus stopped at another hotel, the driver unloaded luggage for some of the disembarking passengers.

"Could you tell me if there's somewhere close by to stay tonight. I mean...somewhere quite cheap?"

The driver looked at Carlos and then climbed back into his seat. Carlos stood up and walked towards the open door of the bus. He stepped out. The sky was reddish in colour and Carlos knew it would be getting dark in a few hours.

"Get back in. I know somewhere."

Carlos got back on the bus and stood next to the driver, firmly holding onto an overhead rail.

"You're travelling alone?"

"Yes. I'm going to walk Saint Paul's pilgrimage to Damascus."

The driver laughed and shook Carlos firmly by the shoulder.

"You're young and crazy but maybe you'll learn something. I know just the place for a pilgrim to stay. It's not far from the New Gate of the old city. It's called the Franciscan House for Pilgrims at Casa Nova. Very appropriate, don't you think?!"

Carlos trudged up the narrow streets towards Casa Nova. He found the Franciscan House a little off the road, surrounded by some palm trees and large pots of green vegetation that wound their way up the building's pale, sandstone walls. He had never stayed in a hotel before and this place did not look like the many hotels and apartments that covered the coast of Cyprus. He went inside to rent a room. The placed bustled with people and he could hear the clanking of cutlery nearby. He looked up at the high, white, arched roof. It was more like a church. Carlos smiled to himself. He knew this was the kind of place where his journey to Damascus should begin.

"You must pay for the room now and with cash, young sir."

Carlos pulled the wad of money Padre Callico had given him from his backpack. The moustached clerk at the reception desk snatched the notes from Carlos' outstretched hand.

He counted the notes carefully and dropped the key of the room onto the reception desk.

"It's number twenty-two, at the rear of the courtyard."

Carlos picked up the key and turned to find his room.

"And sir, you must be out of the room by eleven in the morning."

"So late? I'll be up and gone much earlier than eleven. You see, I've a very important journey ahead of me tomorrow."

That evening, after he had rested and eaten a small dinner of poached eggs and chicken at the Franciscan House, he went out into the streets for a little walk, eventually deciding to sit outside a café and sip on a glass of wine. The owner had first refused to serve him the wine, but when Carlos took out his wad of money and placed some on the table, the owner laughed and re-turned with the wine and some fruit and ice-cream Carlos had not asked for.

"Pardon me, it was my mistake. Enjoy the ice-cream with our compliments."

Carlos sat back in his chair and enjoyed the ice-cream and the cool evening breeze. He felt so far away from Cyprus. It was as if he had left days ago and not that very same morning. He felt he was in control of his own destiny for the first time and he did not want to let go of that feeling.

He heard the rattle of a trader's cart coming up the road. The cart was piled high with boxes of figurines and picture frames. The boxes were tied on with ropes but still swayed to and fro as the wheels of the cart hit each bump in the road. In-evitably, two small wooden boxes careered from the top of the pile. Little blue and white figurines of Our Lady smashed to the ground and the piec-es scattered across the roadside. The trader stopped pushing the cart and roared something blasphemous into the night. Carlos stool up and walked the few paces towards him, intending to help the trader gather up the broken pieces and salvage what remained of his wares. But the trader was quickly joined by an old woman dressed in a long black dress walking behind him. Carlos sat back down at his table outside the café. He did not want to embarrass the trader or cause a fuss and he could still hear him swearing to himself under his breath. After a minute or so, the trader gestured to the old woman to leave him alone. He packed the boxes back on top of the cart and went on his way, leaving many broken pieces of Our Lady on the street.

The old woman seemed a little out of breath. She walked over to the café and sat on a chair close to Carlos. She clutched her head and patted her breast for a moment.

"Are you alright? Can I get you anything? Perhaps some water?"

"No, no, my dear man. You're sweet, but it's age, not thirst!"

She manoeuvred her chair around to face him.

"Are you visiting Jerusalem?"

"Yes, but I'm going to Damascus in the morning."

The old woman smiled at him and released a gentle but deliberate sigh.

"So many have gone there and I'm not sure what they're looking for."

Carlos thought once more about why he had come to Jerusalem.

"I want to walk in the footsteps of Saint Paul, like my Uncle Bakkar did many years ago. I'll be glad when I set out in the morning. I'm not very comfortable in cities. And this place is surrounded by a wall. It's as if people are afraid all the time."

"Oh no, we're afraid of nothing, and I've certainly nothing to be afraid of at my age. You see, there are eight gates around this city, but only one is closed."

Carlos hoped he had not offended the old woman. He felt his head was a little heavy. He had drunk his wine a little too quickly. He looked around and thought it was time to return to the Franciscan House.

"I'm sorry, it's late and I should go. I have a long journey ahead of me."

He stood up and looked in the direction he would walk. The old woman stood up and placed her hand on his shoulder.

"You are a true pilgrim. I can see it in your eyes. But I can also see fear and youth go hand in hand. I beg you, travel safely, and know what you wish for at the end of your pilgrimage."

She walked to the side of the road and then turned around.

"Promise me one thing..."

Carlos got up from his table and walked over to the woman. She held out her arm and Carlos instinctively linked his arm with hers.

"Please, can I walk you home? It's late and you were kind to help that grumpy old trader."

The old woman put her bony finger to her lips. "Shh..."

They turned in the direction of the Franciscan House, walking very slowly.

"Let's walk in whatever direction takes you safely to your bed. This is my city. I know her well. She speaks her wisdom to me when it's late."

He felt the old woman's weight upon his arm. As slowly as they walked, he still sensed the old woman tiring quickly.

"Please, there's no need for this."

"Shh...Enough! Listen to the old city and you will hear every footstep on the stones below our feet. Christ himself walked these very same steps."

She pulled her shawl up over her head when they eventually reached the door of the Franciscan House. She plucked a piece of vegetation growing from the wall of the building and placed it in the palm of his hand.

"It's getting chilly now. Go inside and rest for your journey tomorrow. But promise me something, will you?"

"I will."

"Before you leave the city in the morning, visit the Church of the Holy Sepulchre. It's not far from here. And when you leave the city, you must leave by the Damascus Gate."

She turned and began walking in the direction they had come from.

Carlos shouted after her when he thought she was still in earshot.

"I promise."

She raised a hand to him without turning her head. He watched her disappear into the darkness of the street.

Carlos left the Franciscan House early the next morning. He bought some water and began to look for the Church of the Holy Sepulchre. He carried the green sprig the old woman gave him the night before safely in his trouser pocket. He did not know why he kept the sprig, or why he was going to the church, but he did not want to break his promise to her. She seemed sincere and he thought the church might have some symbolic significance for pilgrims before they set out on their journey.

He found the church close by in the Christian quarter of the city. It was a magnificent stone building capped with two domes, one much larger than the other. A complex series of towers and out-buildings surrounded the main body of the church. He found a crowd of about a hundred people massed outside the main entrance. This was nothing like the church in the centre of the market in Lefkosa. He had to queue for quite a while before finally getting inside. He sat in a seat at the back of the church and admired the fabulous statues and frescoes. People filed past and he saw a look of awe in their faces. Some respectfully blessed themselves, while others fell to their knees and wept uncontrollably. He felt something deep inside him well up, but he could not understand why.

He noticed the old woman he had met the night before sitting a couple of seats ahead of him. She was wearing the same black dress and her shawl was wrapped loosely around her neck. He recognised her long grey hair and bony frame. He did not want to disturb her. She was praying with her head bowed, and when she unclasped her hands, he could see she was clutching tightly a string of rosary beads. When she eventually got up from her seat to leave the church, she saw Carlos, nodded and smiled, and paused at the pew where he was sitting.

"I'm glad you came."

"I promised you I would."

He spent an hour in the church with the old woman. She took him to the large dome and showed him the marble slab that covered the rock where Christ's body lay after his crucifixion. She led him up steps to the place where Christ's cross once stood. She showed him ornate anointing jars hanging on a gold frame and the many altars in the church. She walked him through all the depictions of the Stations of the Cross on the walls of the church. All the time his thoughts were filled with Monika.

"There's one more thing I must show you before you leave for Damascus."

She led him outside the church and for a moment the strong sunlight dazzled his eyes. She gripped his hand firmly in hers and reached up to rub it on the stone wall of the church.

"What do you see on your hand?"

Carlos hesitated because he was a little puzzled by the old woman's actions. He could see a thick layer of golden-white dust in the palm of his hand. She cupped his hand in hers. He could feel her hands trembling.

"We are afraid of nothing. This is what we're protecting inside the walls of this city. We're at the centre of the world. Look carefully at what you hold in the palm of your hand."

She closed his hand tightly within hers.

"This is our history. You will see much of it on your journey. It will dry your throat and burn your face when the winds pick up on the desert plains. You must protect yourself. It's the dust of our history in this city and what we must protect. You will find so much of it on your journey to Damascus."

She let go of his hand gently. He looked at the dust still stuck to the palm of his hand.

"Do you have the sprig I gave you last night?"

Carlos reached into his trouser pocket and took it out to show her.

"When all seems endless and lost, take this sprig and hold it in the palm of your hand. Hold it tightly and don't give it up. Like you, it will one day bloom and guide you to what you cherish most. It will always give you hope and belief."

She sensed Carlos' uneasiness. She gripped his hand again and blew the dust away.

"You see, nothing to be afraid of. Now, bring your hands together and brush away any last grains that remain."

She turned and he watched her walk into the crowd gathered outside the church. Carlos stood for a while drinking some of his bottled water. He realised he did not know the woman's name and she had never enquired about his.

12

He kept his promise to the woman and left the old city through the Damascus Gate. The Damascus Gate was a great stone archway that led out to an ancient Roman amphitheatre. He did not stop to browse among the many market traders' wares laid out on colourful sheets on the steps. He passed a large group of students chattering away in high-pitched voices. He wondered what these students would do with the knowledge and wisdom they were filled with. They were giddy with the magical sites of a fabulous city. They did not notice a young man taking his first steps on the road to Damascus.

Carlos headed eastward on the El-Wad Road, high up into the hills, leaving the bustle of Jerusalem far behind him. The hillsides were covered with the ruins of old battlement towers and small peasant farms and outhouses. He had spent a little time that morning carefully studying his map and marked out his movements for the next eight days with a dark pencil. He knew he must walk a minimum distance every day and he had boldly marked a circle to indicate each day's final destination. Today, he wanted to reach Jericho before the sun set in the west behind the hills. He knew it was important to avoid spending time on the road when the sun was at its hottest in the early afternoons. He was a little angry with himself because he would have to do this on his first day on the road to Damascus. His visit to the Church of the Holy Sepulchre had delayed his departure, but he had not wanted to disappoint the old woman. He had kept his promise and left the city by the Damascus Gate. He consoled himself a little and stopped to drink some water. He needed to push hard today and reach a place of safety and shelter in the evening. There, at least, he could replenish his body and spirit and rest in preparation for an early start the following morning. He knew there would be many more difficult days than today. His map detailed many higher mountains, isolated and rough roads, and great barren, desert plains. Carlos looked at his large bottle of water and he saw it was already less than half full. He was disgusted by his own greed and shoved the bottle inside his backpack. His feet pounded the road ahead and he could feel the water swishing sickeningly inside his stomach. He felt ashamed, not for the first time.

The day grew older and Carlos crossed the Mount of Olives, covered with its dusty bushes and trees, and tramped along the uneven, undulating road through the Wadi Qelt gorge. He grew increasingly tired with every footstep. Finally, the warm sun gave up and began to sink towards the tips of the mountains behind him. He watched the shadows cast by the sun grow longer. The sunlight finally stopped glistening on the waters of the Dead Sea in the distance, far below the hillsides. In the late afternoon, a young Englishman riding a small, noisy motorcycle stopped and offered him a lift. He spoke to Carlos for a few minutes and explained that he was on holidays. Carlos refused his offer. He sped off on his motorcycle, disgruntled, mocking Carlos for his stubbornness.

"You're a fool, young man! We could be in Jericho in twenty minutes, dining on steaks and drinking fine wine."

He arrived in Jericho a while after darkness fell. His feet were sore and blistered from the unevenness of the roads. His throat was dry from the dust and he had long used up all his water. Yet, when he reached Jericho, he did not stop. It was as if his body had grown accustomed to the movement. Carlos felt if he stopped and sat down, his body would weaken further and seize upon the comforts of rest, and he would not be able to deal with the rigours and strains of the coming days. He walked through the square of the city, and finally, his legs went from under him. He stumbled onto his knees under a large palm tree beside a stone water fountain. He reached into the fountain and dowsed his face with the cool water. It was the most wonderful experience he'd ever felt. The droplets teased his lips and his tongue stretched out as if he were about to sip sweet honey. He sat for some time on a small wall beside the fountain and watched the jets of water splashing down. He thought about steaks and fine, rich, red wine. He should have taken the offer of a lift from the Englishman. He wondered how Saint Paul could possibly have walked all the way from Jerusalem to Damascus.

He found a room to stay in above an old pottery workshop, owned by a young fruit trader on the outskirts of the city. Carlos had met him in the square and bought fruit from his stall.

"You won't find anywhere to stay so late in the evening, young Carlos. I'm happy to help a young traveller."

Carlos helped the trader pack up his stall and they carried some boxes back to his stone cottage at the edge of the city. They put away the boxes in a wooden shed at the side of the cottage and sat down on the side of the road. Saffri, the fruit seller, lit a cigarette, drew in a deep breath, and savoured his day's work.

"You look weary. You should rest tomorrow."

"I can't Saffri. I have to get to Damascus in eight days."

"Eight days...walking?"

"Yes, like Saint Paul, and his pilgrimage to destroy Christianity."

"Are you planning the same thing, Carlos?"

"No, Saffri!"

Carlos stood up and walked a little way out to the centre of the road. He buried his hands deep inside his trouser pockets. He did not feel Saffri was taking him seriously.

"My Uncle Bakkar walked the same journey many years ago. It changed him. He became bitter and gave up his studies at a monastery in Cyprus. I lived a year with him in the mountains herding goats, and he even gave up on that."

"Sometimes you just have to find the right place, Carlos. It takes time. You can travel to all the places you want and never find out what settles your spirit."

Carlos walked back towards Saffri.

"You're tired, Carlos."

"I'm not!"

Carlos stopped. Saffri glared at him for a moment and then smiled.

"Not only are you tired, Carlos, you're a little angry and stubborn."

Carlos slumped back down on the side of the road beside Saffri and placed his head in his hands. Saffri slapped Carlos playfully on the back and stood up.

"Come on. Let's go inside."

Carlos followed Saffri into the small cottage. All sorts of pots and pans hung from large wooden timbers in the roof. Saffri lit some candles and they sat on two stools beside the only window in the cottage.

"I was brought up in Armenia, and when I was eight, there was a very big earthquake in my country. Thousands upon thousands died in the cities and the many houses built on the hillsides. I lived with my mother and father on a farm in the countryside. But what was more terrible than the 'quake was the thousands of deaths afterwards. The countryside filled with people from the mountainside villages and small towns. They headed for the farmlands in the hope of getting food and shelter and stayed in makeshift campsites. It happened a little time before the bitterly cold winter months. When you're starving, winter seems to come a lot quicker. I've seen dead lambs, goats, but the sight of a young woman and her newborn child, dead, lying sodden for weeks in a ditch, still clutching her child...well, it just..."

Saffri stopped telling his story of the earthquake. He was silent for a while. Carlos could see his face in the candlelight. He could see the pain of Saffri's family, his people, and his country.

"We left Armenia. My mother had been unwell for several months, right through the winter. She never made it to Israel with us. The hardest thing wasn't leaving her when she died, but burying her in a common grave with so many others. We travelled on a simple horse and cart with all our possessions. Finally, we just had to stop somewhere, and we found this place. We decided we had to stop looking for something we may never have found, no matter how long we travelled. We left Armenia; firstly, because we felt we had to. Our farm was destroyed by bandits and our herds slaughtered. But secondly, and most importantly, we left because there was nothing for us in Armenia. No matter where we went, we still knew we'd always be Armenians. My father decided to visit my mother's grave a week ago. I couldn't stop him leaving. How could I? I fear the worst now. Maybe he won't come back here. I just don't know. But I know his heart has been broken since we lost my mother."

Carlos began to think about his own mother and father.

"I lost both of my parents to illness. I lived for a while with my uncle in the mountains. We herded goats there. We talked late into the evenings but it's only recently that I realised how little I knew about my uncle."

"Did he know about you going on this pilgrimage?"

"No, he woke the morning I planned to leave and then disappeared. He didn't know about my pilgrimage. I just told him I'd decided to leave. We both knew the time had come. And the morning I left. I discovered he gave away the herd to a Syrian farmer and his sons in the market. But before I left for Israel, I found out he had made the same pilgrimage when he was studying religious theology at a monastery. I suppose it made it easier to leave Cyprus, like it was also somehow my purpose to come here."

Carlos did not mention the journals because he was still ashamed of Bakkar.

They talked long into the night, and before Carlos knew it, the light of the early morning crept through the small window of the cottage. Saffri walked to the window and opened it a little. Carlos got up from his chair. He could feel the stiffness and soreness of his legs. He stretched out and then sat back down. He rubbed the backs of his legs, his ankles, and then his blistered feet. Carlos could feel the cool refreshing breeze on his face from the open window.

"Carlos, I'm sorry I've kept you up so long. We should get some sleep before the sun rises properly and it gets warmer."

Saffri blew out the single candle still burning and lay down on a small bed.

"There are sheets in the cupboard and a heavy blanket to sleep on."

Carlos walked to the window and watched the sunrise for a while. He would have to set out soon, but his body felt so tired. He knew he had to lie down for a while. He sat with his back against the wall under the window, but he could not settle. Finally, his mind and body gave in and he crept over to the foot of Saffri's bed and lay awkwardly across it, salvaging what rest and comfort he could.

He dreamed about Saffri's journey from Armenia to Israel on a rickety horse and cart and each bump on the road as it wound its way along perilous mountainsides. He could hear the howl of the harsh winds and the whimpering of starving children and the cries of mothers and fathers.

He awoke some hours later, still stretched across Saffri's legs. He jumped up from the bed and staggered to the window. He could feel the warmth of the noon sun outside. Saffri stirred in his bed and sat upright. Carlos slumped to the floor and tried to stifle his sobs.

"I can't do this, Saffri. I should be walking along the shores of the River Jordan right now."

Carlos pulled his backpack over to him and took out his map. He rubbed the tears from his cheeks and threw the map on the floor. Saffri got out of bed and quickly dressed. He knelt beside Carlos, picked up the map, and studied it for a while.

"If it's not long after noon then I know someone who might be able to get you as far as Beit She'an."

He waved the map in front of Carlos, stabbing his finger at a point on it.

Saffri went to the door and opened it.

"Quickly, wash yourself and I'll be back very soon."

Saffri returned a few minutes later. He was out of breath and rushed over to Carlos who was sitting on the bed clutching his backpack. Saffri reached inside his shirt and took out a large orange.

"A late breakfast! Come on, you can eat it on the way."

They met an old fruit wholesaler called Khaleb sitting in his truck in the market square. They sat with him in the cab of his truck while he feverishly spooned a can of cold beans into his mouth.

"Khaleb has been delivering fruit to this market since he was my age. He doesn't speak much English so you'll be able to catch up on some lost sleep."

Saffri clamoured out of the cab and stood on the footpath.

"Take care of my friend, Khaleb, and remember the place he wants to go."

"Yes, yes, Saffri. Beit She'an."

Khaleb flung the empty can on the dashboard and started the truck. Carlos jumped out and hugged Saffri.

"Thank you for what you've done."

Saffri stood back and looked uneasily up and down the street.

"It's nothing Carlos. Go on, before the old fool gets any grumpier and changes his mind. He'll get you to Beit She'an and you'll have gained nearly a full day on your journey. Go and do whatever it is you've got to do."

Carlos watched Saffri through the cracked side mirror on the truck. He faded into a cloud of dust. Carlos gripped his backpack tightly to his chest and soon his eyes grew heavy and the rumble of the engine set him off to sleep.

When you journey, you must always travel with your soul and your spirit; without them, you will become quickly lost. Remember how you felt as a young boy when the trees took you into their bows and you felt your mother's spirit close beside you. You can only take the comforts of the soul on a long journey. Ask yourself; what are you taking with you? What are you leaving behind? But most importantly; what do you wish to find at the end of your journey? When you understand truly what you have left behind, then you will understand what it is you need to take with you. If you do not know these things already, then you will never understand why you are on the road. You will be destined to return empty-handed. Your spirit will be broken and your soul will have learnt nothing. When you undertake life's journey, thread purposefully, but honestly, and you will disturb nothing, only the desires you wish to awaken.

Carlos walked a little way down a slope off the main road and settled himself under a cluster of olive trees. He had slept in the cab of the truck all day until Khaleb woke him when they reached Beit She'an. Khaleb had refused the money Carlos offered him, but instead, the grumpy old driver just pointed at the large orange and Carlos was happy to part with it as payment for a good deed.

For the first time in two days, Carlos felt alert and refreshed. He could not feel any stiffness or soreness in his legs anymore. He breathed in the late afternoon air and gazed down on a small village below the hillside. He could hear the odd car pass by on the main road above him. He lay back and looked at the clear sky before his eyes. He could hear a dog persistently barking in the distance. He thought about the words Tass had spoken to him in a dream earlier that afternoon. For a moment, he could smell the pine trees in the forests at the foot of the Troodos Mountains, and when he closed his eyes, he could see Monika's young, pretty face. He had left nothing else behind him. Padre Callico's words and advice were clear in his thoughts, and in a forest close to his home village, two trees held true the spirit and memories of his mother and father. He kept their souls deep in his heart. He knew where the road ahead would take him, but as every hour and day passed, he wondered truly why he had embarked on the road to Damascus and what he would find there, if anything. He knew why Saint Paul had set out on his journey to Damascus, but like his Uncle Bakkar, Carlos had simply set out on his journey through some instinctive conviction. Yet, Carlos already felt he had somehow cheated. He had turned down the offer of a lift from the Englishman but succumbed through physical exhaustion to accepting a lift to Beit She'an with Khaleb, the grumpy truck driver. It was foolish, but he had felt such an affinity with Saffri and his tragic journey from Armenia. It made his own pilgrimage to Damascus seem fanciful when so many others before him had walked the same road as a sign and gift of their spiritual devotion to God.

He sat up, picked up his backpack, and decided he would walk a little farther before the light of the day began to fade. He remembered the last few words spoken by Tass in his dream.

When you undertake life's journey, thread purposefully, but honestly, and you will disturb nothing, only the desires you wish to awaken.

Carlos walked casually along the road. He was a little ahead of time on his journey to Damascus. There seemed no need to hurry or push his body and he reflected on the many wonderful and breathtaking sights he had already passed by. The charming farms and the ruins of churches covered the countryside, but he had not wanted to stop. When he passed someone standing or sitting by the roadside, he had simply nodded to acknowledge them out of courtesy. The words of Tass kept ringing in his head. He mouthed the words silently to himself. He knew what he had to do.

13

It was the first time Carlos had taken one of the journals from his backpack since he'd left Cyprus. He had crossed over the River Jordan into Syria just south of the Sea of Galilee. He sat on a hilltop in the shade of some tall bushes and watched the rays of the midday sun glisten on the waters of the sea in the distance. He was three and a half days into his journey to Damascus. The land was sandy and barren. Soon, he would be trekking through the most dangerous and exhausting landscape on his journey to Damascus. When he looked out onto the arid landscape, a feeling of uneasiness filled him.

He opened the first blank page of the journal and slowly and purposefully began to write. His mind had been taken over and filled with dreams over the past two nights and his hand quickened as he scribbled down the images and words from those dreams. At times, he paused and looked up from the page, as if he had been disturbed by a passer-by. It was as if his hand and mind were taken over by some force beyond him and he had to struggle to keep up. Occasionally, he would stop scribbling in the journal and his eyes would focus on something far away in the distance. Then, he would hear a word spoken by Tass, and his mind and hand would stir feverishly on the page once again.

The elders and wise men sat in a circle in a small clearing shadowed by the giant trees. Each one, in turn, slowly closed his eyes and thought about the dreams of the passing night. Though each man's eyes were now tightly shut, they could still see the shape, texture and colour of every leafy creature surrounding them. Through their noses they could still breathe the fresh smell of the forest, and through their ears, they could still hear the wind in the branches of the trees. However, this morning, one of the wise men was not thinking of the trees, nor was he thinking of the dreams of the passing night. He was thinking of his son.

Carlos looked up again from his journal. Though his hand twitched with eagerness to write, he knew he needed to return to the road. He closed the journal and put it away in his backpack. The sun was still warm and it was at its highest point in the sky. He walked up a steep slope and found his way back onto the road. He walked with the banks of the River Jordan to his left side.

By late afternoon Carlos rested again by the roadside and a man on a donkey stopped beside him. He climbed down from the donkey and led the animal down to the banks of the river to drink. He left the donkey by the water and returned up the bank to where Carlos was sitting. He wore white shrouds and a red scarf wrapped heavily around his face. He carried a short metal pole in one hand and a cloth bag in the other hand. He sat near Carlos and spoke in a tongue Carlos could not understand. Carlos was sure he was Arabic. He was sure he was an elder and his face was cracked like worn leather from the heat of the sun. The man reached into his cloth bag and took out half a loaf of bread. He ripped it in two and held out one piece to Carlos.

"Eat, eat!"

Carlos took the bread and smiled warmly at the man. They sat in silence, and later shared a bottle of water Carlos had in his backpack. The donkey came up from the banks of the river and stood beside them, shuffling and kicking its hooves into the sand. The elder began to sing to himself in a low droning voice that steadily became louder and louder, until Carlos could hear his beautiful poignant voice echo back at them from the surrounding hills. Finally, the elder stood up, stretched out his limbs to the world, and walked to his donkey. He pointed at Carlos and slapped the back of the donkey with his hand.

"Up, up!"

Carlos hesitated for a moment. The elder slapped the donkey repeatedly until Carlos quickly stood up and gathered his water and backpack. He pulled Carlos up onto the rear of the donkey and they set out along the road. They moved slowly for almost two hours until they passed through a small valley between two high mountains. They dismounted the donkey and the elder took a rolled up rug which he had used as a saddle and spread it out on the cool sand. Carlos knew they would have to rest and sleep out in the open for a night or two because the desert region was so barren and uninhabited.

They sat together on the rug as the light of the day faded. Carlos took out his map to study it as best he could in the poor evening light. The elder seemed inquisitive and ran his fingers over the map before looking at Carlos. Carlos pointed at Jerusalem and ran his finger all the way to Damascus. The elder seemed to understand and he smiled and nodded. He took hold of the map from Carlos and pointed to Tiberias on the coast of the Sea of Galilee. He pounded the palm of his hand against his chest and grasped Carlos' hand. The elder led Carlos' finger from Tiberias northward along the map to a tiny place deep into Syria called Ghabaghib. He let go of Carlos and pounded his chest once again. Carlos understood too. He thought they might become kindred travelling spirits of the mountains.

They gathered some dry wood and lit a fire in the evening. It was cold, far colder than any night Carlos had experienced on the road to Damascus. They lay back and slept with the fire crackling at their feet. Carlos dreamed again. He dreamed of the elders and wise men of his village. He dreamed of burning bushes in the desert and warriors fighting with swords on the banks of the River Jordan. He dreamed of the road ahead to Damascus, and when his mind tired, he slept soundly under the clear moonlight.

The sun had risen high when he awoke but the elder still slept soundly beside him. Carlos was aware of a haze filling the valley. It shimmered and he struggled to clearly focus on anything. He could just about make out a shadow of a figure approaching from a distance. He thought about waking the elder, but he was still unsure if they were in any danger. The figure grew steadily closer but became no clearer to him in the shimmer of heat. Carlos wiped the sleep from his eyes and stood up to greet the approaching stranger. He felt an ominous and uneasy feeling grow deep inside him. He remembered Padre Callico's words of warning to be careful, particularly in the remoteness of the desert plains. He stepped forward a little and walked into a rising and swirling wind. The wind flapped and buffeted his clothes wildly. He struggled to steady himself. The wind grew fiercer and grains of sand filled the air like tiny fragments of glass. He fell to his knees and wrapped his arms around his head to protect his eyes and face. The sandstorm grew more powerful, and as he dared to peer out beyond his sheltering arms, he could see the sands slowly gathering around his feet, and then his legs. He could not move anymore. He slumped down into the sand and continued to cover his head as best he could. The wind howled incessantly like a crazed wolf in his ears. He screamed out for the elder to come and help him but Carlos could not even hear the sound of his own voice above the wind. He lifted his face from the sand and saw a figure standing over him. The howling wind began to carry a voice. He struggled to hear it for a while. In an instant, the wind died down. He dared again to lift his head from the sand but he could feel his eyes sting from the grains in the wind. He reached out to wipe them with his hands, but they too were covered in sand. He strained to see the shadowy figure standing over him. He heard the voice clearly, and in that moment he knew it was his father. Though he wanted to reach out to him, his whole body was gripped with fear.

Carlos. We talked so much about honour, respect, love, yet all the time, love was left until last. I never told you how much I loved you. I never let you tell me how much you loved me. You honoured and respected me. You honoured and respected the elders and wise men of our village, through the practice of wisdom and learning. You meant so much to the elders of our village. They saw in you a quality it takes many years to understand and achieve. Yet, in your own way, you challenged every boundary your mother and I set for you. If I could hold you now, I wouldn't let go, but I know this isn't what you need. Now I'm gone, though I can see you, I can't touch you or hold you, and this is the way it should be. If I could, my love would crush you with its strength. When we lived together as a family, we obeyed the rules of our people, even in weakness and sickness. I understand, and only now, when a father teaches his son honour and respect, there forms a certain distance between the two of them. But I've come to respect that you are no longer trapped by our people and our village. When I watch you, I truly have come to know who you really are. When we were together in the earthly world, we spoke easily about love, but we didn't show it enough. I have only these words for you, and not the arms to wrap around your body in the midst of the sandstorm. Though my image in your eyes may turn and go, I'll always be here waiting for you. Take all the time you need, but don't ever be sad in this world for a single day.

The wind grew strong again. Carlos desperately tried to fix his eyes on the departing shadowy figure, but he could not help but try to protect his face and eyes from the stinging grains of sand. It took forever for the winds to die down. Carlos began to scold himself because he had not stood up to see if the ghost truly was his father. He was angry with himself, but he also felt ashamed. He kept his head down and his arms covered his face until he could no longer hear or feel the wind. He struggled to free his legs and feet from the layers of sand covering them. He dusted himself off and scanned the horizon around him. It was as if nothing had ever happened.

He was amazed to find the elder still fast asleep on the unfurled rug. He dropped to his knees and shook the elder until he woke.

"Did you not hear the sandstorm? I've seen my father! He came here to the desert and spoke to me."

The elder glared at Carlos, still rubbing his eyes and steadying himself as he sat up. He frowned and grumbled something to himself while pushing Carlos' arms away. Carlos gave up. Even if the elder understood him, he would never believe him. The elder rolled up the rug and they both gathered their things. All the time, Carlos kept looking at the distant horizon, hoping he might catch a glimpse of the shadowy figure again.

They journeyed north in silence and the elder did not sing once that day. His mood seemed to have changed. They finally stopped on a sloping plain where several men on camels had pitched some small tents. The elder dismounted the donkey and greeted the men warmly. The men in turn all embraced the elder. They seem to know each other. Carlos felt a little uneasy but decided to follow the elder over to where they had all sat around a camp fire. He sat close to the elder, but none of the other men greeted him. He had sat in meditation and study with the elders and wise men of his own village many times, but this was different. He did not understand their ways or what bonded all these men together. Soon, he saw their knives and guns. The elder got up and fetched a cloth sack strapped to the donkey. He emptied the contents out on the sand in front of the men. The men cheered and laughed at the treasures laid out on the sand. Carlos could see the sparkle of necklaces, rings, brooches, coins and lockets of every size and description. They sparkled magnificently in the sunlight. He had never seen so many precious and fabulous jewels like these. Like a horde of skilled merchant jewellers at a market, the men huddled around the gems on their knees and held them up to their eyes, carefully examining every contour and detail. The men handed wads of money to the elder and took some of the jewellery. Eventually the elder gathered up the remaining jewellery and placed it back in the cloth sack. He dropped the sack at Carlos' feet, grunted and pointed to the donkey. Carlos felt deceived by the elder. He knew then the elder was just a wild old thief, and nothing more.

Carlos tied the sack onto the donkey. He did not trust any of the men. He returned to the camp fire. One of the men was preparing the carcass of a lamb to cook. He stripped the skin from the lamb with a long knife and violently drove a wooden pole through its body with a mallet before placing it onto a spit above the fire. They sat around the fire until it was dark and ate the meat with some bread and goat's milk. The elder and the men smoked from small wooden pipes after they ate. They talked and laughed loudly and never once spoke to Carlos that night. Carlos wanted to be back on the road to Damascus on his own. He felt trapped and alone out in the desert with these men. He could not talk to them and he feared he was becoming a part of a band of thieves and vagabonds. Worse, he feared they were travelling bandits, and when he listened to his heart, it spoke only of danger. Carlos knew he had to escape them.

It was quiet and daylight was still a little way off. Most of the men were sleeping in their tents. He took out his journal and began to write. The elder was still awake smoking his pipe. Carlos could feel the eyes of the elder watching him as he wrote. He filled a full page, but then the words stopped coming from inside him. He could not hear the voice of Tass, so he pretended to write, hoping the elder would soon fall asleep. Instead, the elder got up, walked over to Carlos, and gesticulated for Carlos to hand him the journal. Carlos shook his head. The elder pulled some rings and coins from his pocket and held them out to Carlos. Carlos shook his head again. The elder grew angry and threw the rings and coins at Carlos. They hit him in the face and he recoiled backwards. He sat up and put the journal into his backpack. The elder began hissing and shouting at Carlos in Arabic and tried to grab the backpack from him. Carlos leapt to his feet. He felt a blow across the side of his face as the elder swung his fist out. He staggered along the sand, half running and half crawling on his hands and knees. Finally, he managed to stay on his feet and he ran as fast as he could into the blackness of the desert night. He wanted to run all the way to Damascus, but after what seemed like an age, his legs could not run any farther, and his heart felt like it was about to explode out of his chest. He collapsed in a heap, desperate to catch his breath. He looked back in the direction he had run from and hoped the elder would not try and follow him. He listened in the darkness for any sign he was being pursued, but he could only hear the beating of his heart.

Carlos slept for a little while in the hollow of a sand dune. He awoke with the rising sun beating down on his tired body. He pulled his map out from his backpack and tried to work out where he was. He knew he was less than a day's walk from Nawa, but he would have to avoid the main travel route, fearing the elder would catch up with him on the way to Ghabaghib farther north. He needed to get to Nawa by the end of the day. He had no water or food with him and he feared the journey would be exhausting and difficult. His lip was a little swollen. He touched it with his fingers and saw flakes of dried blood on his fingertips. He vowed to himself that he would travel alone for the rest of the journey to Damascus. He was annoyed with himself for letting mistrust into his heart, but he had no choice. If another person stopped him on the road to Damascus, he would shun them.

14

He walked for miles that day and the desert road gave way to a green oasis of bushes and trees. He reached the city of Nawa by early evening and found a room at a hostel. He was sure he had escaped the elder and the bandits in the desert. He was happy to walk among the crowds of locals and tourist in the streets. He felt bad about losing his trust in people because of one person who had treated him poorly. He had met so many people who had offered him help and advice since he set out from Cyprus on the road to Damascus. He thought it was sad how sometimes one man's actions can somehow colour the view of everyone. His experience in the desert with the elder made him think of the journey of Saint Paul to Damascus. He knew every journey changes a man, no matter how long or short the road travelled. He knew from the words of Tass that what you seek on a journey is not necessarily what you will find at the end of the journey. Saint Paul set out for Damascus filled with a conviction to destroy Christianity, yet, he left Damascus with Christianity in his heart.

The hostel was a noisy place at night. The floors of the corridors were made of stone and he could hear the sound of footsteps constantly coming and going. He tried to write in his journal for a while under the light of a small bedside lamp. His eyes hurt, so he lay back and listened to doors slamming and the sound of voices, some Arabic, some English, echo through the corridors. The voices slowly blended together and his ear started to become more accustomed to them. Soon, he believed he could understand every foreign word spoken. He knew their stories and they echoed his own story. Perhaps they were going to Damascus too.

He was not sure if he had drifted off into a light sleep, but when he opened his eyes, it was quieter. The voices had merged into one voice, and this voice was soft to his ears. It was the softness of a woman's voice, barely audible, whispering away to him in the darkness. He strained to hear it properly.

I love you.

He sat up in bed. The soft whisper was close-by, not outside in the corridor, but there, beside him in the room.

I love you, yet, I don't know you now. I left you when you were so young, when you accepted every kiss and hug. I don't know you as you are now, Carlos, making your own way in the world. I never knew you when you could be hurt, when you felt alone, because your father and I were always there when you were young. I hugged and kissed you all the time, yet, you need a hug and kiss so much more now. I hope all I gave you will keep you safe and warm all the days of your life. I know how much you think of me, but remember, I'm always with you, in every breath, through every pain, in everything you see, hear and feel.

Carlos heard the words clearly. He knew it was his mother's voice. He looked into the darkness but could see nothing. He felt a sudden draught from the window which rattled the door of the room. He was sad because he had not seen his mother, but he could smell her scent in the room, a wonderful mix of fresh roses and olives. He breathed the aroma in and it made him smile, and though he felt the tears in his eyes, his heart was smiling. He could still smell the olives, and it made him not only think of his mother, but of Monika back in Cyprus.

He set out from Nawa with a renewed confidence and with every footstep he tread in the sand, he knew he was not alone. He walked along a small road which he knew would take him to a little town called Jasim. He planned to rest there for a couple of hours, away from the glare and heat of the midday sun. Ghabaghid was nearly twice the distance farther north and he was unsure if he could make it that far before nightfall. If he didn't, then he would have to risk sleeping under the stars. Though he was uneasy about this, he knew his money was dwindling, and he would need to keep some money when he reached Damascus to pay for the bus back to the boat. He thought about beautiful Cyprus and the Troodos Mountains. It was the first time he was sure he really wanted to return home.

Shortly after midday, he stopped and sat under the shade of a stone farmhouse and munched on some pears. The lush juice of the fruit stung the cut on his lip. It was pleasant and warm and the sweetness in the air had attracted some bees from a nearby bush. He flapped his hand at them, but they persisted, until finally he rose to his feet, stretched his arms and back and looked for somewhere else to rest. He walked farther down past the farm and found a small stone wall to sit on. He took out his journal and began to write.

Again, the words flowed easily, and he quickly filled several pages. He wondered where the words were coming from. He had never tried to write in the way he had written in the past week and yet it was easy—the words flowed from the pencil to the page as if his hand was overtaken by some natural current inside him. It reminded him of the way a river flowed, outward and onward, unstoppable. Like the waters of a river flowing from the high mountains out to the sea, he could not stop it. He knew he could not cast himself into a small vessel and try to row against the current up into the mountains. It was exciting, but it was also frightening. He understood Bakkar and the journals a little more now. Once Carlos had accepted them into his life, once he placed his mark upon the journal, it consumed him, and he became a part of the words. They were as much his story as history itself. He understood what Bakkar had meant when he said he was writing history.

He closed the journal and placed it safely back in his backpack. The current of the river still flowed through him. He could not stop it. And a part of him did not want to.

He had walked nearly eighteen hours the previous day and reached Ghabaghid before midnight. He found rest and shelter overnight in a small room above a Lebanese restaurant. The kind owner had seen him stagger through the street while he was locking up for the night. The owner had been so disturbed by Carlos' exhaustion that he had helped him inside the restaurant, given him food and let him rest upstairs for the night.

When Carlos awoke, for a moment, he could not remember how he got to the small bed he was lying in. He raised himself up and felt his body aching all over. Then he remembered the kindness the owner had shown him. He washed in a small sink in the corner of the room and dressed.

The owner was sitting at one of his restaurant tables writing in a ledger when Carlos went downstairs. He saw Carlos and stood up. A broad smile crept across his round, moustached face. He was a large, stout man. He walked over to Carlos, limping from one foot to the other.

Carlos felt uneasy and awkward about the restaurant owner's hospitality.

"I didn't mean to cause you any trouble. Thank you for letting me rest here last night."

The owner put his arm around Carlos' shoulder. Carlos could feel the weight of the burly man's arm on the sore muscles in his back.

"You had me worried last night. I thought you were one of those drunken, crazy kids. You were delirious with tiredness."

The owner led Carlos to a table by the window. "Come, sit. It's Carlos, isn't it?"

"Yes, I'm Carlos. I've come from Cyprus."

"Of course, and let me see now, you are on the road to Damascus, or was that the delirium last night, eh?"

The owner laughed out loud and went to fetch some spring water from a large jug on another table. He poured it into a glass and set it in front of Carlos.

"So, it wasn't the delirium? You really are walking the pilgrim's path on foot to Damascus? You may not have been drunk last night, but you are crazy! But also young and very noble. The foothills and the plains in this area are filled with nomads and bandits, the most unscrupulous spirits alive. You must be very careful. This isn't a place for a good young man walking on his own. Are you a believer? Do you have faith?"

"I'm not sure. I think there's a God."

Carlos was not even convinced by his own words.

"My uncle walked the same pilgrimage many years ago. And I had the blessing of Padre Callico from the monastery in Cyprus. He told me about Saint Paul's journey to Damascus."

The owner paced awkwardly up and down the restaurant, still limping from foot to foot. He finally pulled out a chair and sat down beside Carlos.

"But I still don't understand."

Right then, even Carlos did not understand why he was doing what he was doing.

"People take the road to Damascus because they are ill or they're troubled and seek salvation from themselves or they're dedicated men of God. But you, Carlos...why? Last night, you looked like you were trying to drive your body to the grave. Your whole life lies ahead of you and, yet, you drive yourself into danger and exhaustion. For what sacrifice?"

Carlos thought about what the owner said. He fetched his backpack from his room and returned to the same table by the window in the restaurant. The owner was busy preparing food in the kitchen. Carlos felt it was time to leave. He studied his map for a while. He would reach Damascus in about another day and a half. It seemed an age since he left Cyprus and not a morning had passed him by without him thinking of his homeland. He dreamed about walking in the magnificent Troodos Mountains and resting under the great trees to write in his journal. Most of all, he dreamed about Monika. He wanted to tell her about everything that had happened on the road to Damascus. He wanted to tell her about the people he had met and the way he truly felt about her. But he did not know if she would listen to him and understand why he left and whether she would have any time for him if she studied to become a nurse. Carlos grew uneasy. He wanted to be back with her in Cyprus soon. At least then he could try and explain himself. He was filled with so many things he wanted to say to her, so much he had not said to her; the more he thought about what he had not said to her, the farther away Damascus seemed. He had never felt this way about a girl. It was like she had always been in his life, but all their meetings were such fleeting moments.

He went to the kitchen and thanked the owner of the restaurant.

"You have been very kind to me. What is your name?"

The owner was slicing some vegetables. He did not look at Carlos. Instead, he studied the carefully diced cubes of potato and carrot. Carlos turned and walked to the door.

"You don't need to know my name. We will never see each other again. What would be the point in knowing? You'll have walked many roads before I'm long gone from this world."

Carlos stepped out into the bustling street and began walking the road to Damascus. He heard a voice calling after him. He turned to see the owner standing in the doorway of the restaurant.

"Carlos, remember what I said."

Carlos waved to the owner.

"It's Ahab."

The owner went back inside his restaurant and Carlos never did see him again.

Carlos had only just resumed walking when he heard Tass speak to him.

Carlos. You have travelled to this place in the shadow of others who have gone before you. You believe you are ready to discover your path in life, and that you will find your true destiny and purpose when you reach Damascus. I have watched you, from afar, believing in the memory of trees and learning all you could in The Palace of Dreams. You have sat with the wisest men of your village and you have learnt from their wisdom. You are wise, but you know nothing about living with wisdom. You cast it out like a fisherman's net into the depths of the world, gathering and pulling in anything in its wake. A wise man who uses wisdom well, who lives a life of understanding, knows when to cast his net and where the most fruitful waters are. Only then will he draw his net in. You use your wisdom blindly, but you are still young. Do not be discouraged. Something wonderful is going to happen.

Although Carlos wanted to go back to Cyprus, he was afraid the final part of his journey to Damascus might be the most important. He had travelled so far; it seemed pointless to stop now. He wanted something wonderful to happen, but he was afraid nothing would. Padre Callico had told him about Bakkar's disillusionment when he returned after travelling on the road to Damascus. Perhaps something wonderful only happened for a select few pligrims, like Saint Paul.

Carlos walked the dusty road out of Ghabaghib. He sensed a lack of purpose in his footsteps; each stride became heavier. Throughout the day, he found himself continuously stopping to rest. He sipped slowly on his water because he thought he did not deserve it. He never opened his journal, and he felt guilty because of it. He felt he was dishonouring Bakkar and Padre Callico. In his heart, he knew the restaurant owner was right. He had wasted his time travelling on the road to Damascus. It was simply not the right time in his life. He felt stupid and foolish.

15

The old man wanted to walk with Carlos along the road to Damascus. He had been walking behind Carlos for many hours but Carlos had taken no notice of him. Carlos felt pity for the old man walking under the heat of the day's sun and stopped to offer him some water. He held out the bottle when the old man finally caught up with him.

"I'm Carlos. Do you speak English or Greek?"

"I speak many languages because I am a teacher. It will be English today."

"And can I ask your name?"

"Forgive me, but I have heard my name a million times in my lifetime. I can do without hearing it uttered once more."

The old man graciously took the bottle from Carlos and began to drink a little from it. Then he handed it back and smiled.

"That, Carlos, is the second most refreshing thing today. The first was when I rose with the sun."

They walked along the road to Damascus for some time, chatting casually about the beautiful countryside around them. Carlos told the old man a little about Cyprus, the loss of his parents, and the village where he had grown up. When they stopped to rest again, the old man refused to drink any more water. He explained to Carlos why he was on the road to Damascus.

"I am going to meet a very good friend who is ill. It may be the last time I get to see him. And why are you on this road, Carlos?"

"I wanted to prove to myself that I could do it, but most of all I wanted to honour the journey my uncle and Saint Paul took to Damascus."

"You mean you wanted to honour the road to Damascus as a journey, or the pilgrims who previously walked its path?"

Carlos didn't answer the old man because now he knew the road to Damascus was not about boyish adventure or honour. *You came here for yourself and for no one else.* He felt he didn't deserve to be there and he was not worthy, unlike some other pilgrims who had walked the road before him.

The old man studied Carlos' face.

"And Carlos, I must ask if you really know why your uncle and Saint Paul walked the road to Damascus?"

"Well, I thought I did."

"Really?"

"Like them, I want to see everything in the world, all the wonderful things. I want to know all I can. At least, I thought I did."

Carlos thought for a moment, but his head seemed heavy and empty.

"This is just one single road, one journey, and many travel here for different reasons. You should only be here to honour your life and journey, and not the lives and journeys of others. Otherwise, the road will simply wear your body and soul down, and you will not have the reason, will or passion to keep going. What about all the other things in your life you left behind to come here?"

"The other things?"

"Yes, Carlos. There's love, friends and the experience of life itself. All these things are woven together in our lives. You know, Carlos, I can see your spirit, right this very moment. It's like a spring lamb running in the meadows, but it doesn't truly know why it's running. It might be fear and it might be joy. It hasn't learnt its true purpose—its destiny. Your own furtive spirit moves far too quickly."

The old man peered into the distance ahead of them and then he returned his gaze to Carlos.

"I may be able to help you, Carlos."

"Really. How?"

Carlos' eyes lit up. He could not believe he had met such an extraordinary person and he was fascinated that the old man spoke such wisdom like the men in his village. But most of all, Carlos was fascinated by the old man's claim that he could actually see his spirit. The old man began walking slowly up and down in front of Carlos. Carlos thought he was agitated so he tried not to stare at him. The old man walked right up to Carlos and touched him softly on the check with his hand.

"Carlos, the road to Damascus is filled with pilgrims, charlatans, magicians, bandits, saints and sinners alike, but I'm going to show you something few living people see on this road or during their entire lives. I'm going to show you something you cannot buy, steal or learn. I'm going to show you the light in your heart. I'm going to show you the very soul it illuminates. Just like my ill friend I am travelling to see, we all live for just a short time in this earthly world without ever meeting our soul. It is what brings so many people onto the road to Damascus. Today, I am going to show you your soul; something usually only seen in the heavens. Are you sure you would like to see it?"

"Yes, of course I want to see it. Who wouldn't want to see something few have ever experienced on this earth!"

Carlos hardly paused to think when he answered the old man. Maybe this was the real reason he was here. It would be like every book in The Palace of Dreams revealing every word to him in a single precious moment. It would be like every sage, elder and wise man revealing their secrets and experiences to him.

Though his heart opened and his spirit was lifted by what the old man said he could reveal to Carlos, he was still filled with doubt. Even if the old man had the gift and power to do what he claimed, he was unsure if he really wanted to see his own soul and the light that illuminated his heart.

"So, are you truly ready?"

Carlos could feel his heart pounding in his chest and as each second went by like an eternity, he was worried the old man might just be an old travelling trickster.

The old man turned his back on Carlos and began walking up and down again. After a few moments, he beckoned to Carlos with a wave of his arm.

"Come with me."

They left the road and walked higher up into the mountains. The valley below slowly revealed itself to them while they climbed the steep inclines. The old man guided Carlos to the edge of a large precipice. He asked Carlos to listen carefully. They stood quietly above the valley on the mountaintop, but as hard as Carlos tried, he could hear nothing. And all the time the old man smiled, twitched his face, grimaced and talked quietly to himself. He suddenly grabbed Carlos excitedly by the shoulders.

"Now, now, do you hear them?"

But Carlos could hear nothing. The old man pointed to two small birds above them in a tree.

"Don't you hear them talking to each other?"

Carlos could hear the two birds chirping away happily, but he could not understand their words.

"I don't know what they're saying."

The old man shook Carlos a little.

"But can't you just imagine?"

As hard as he tried, Carlos could not understand the language of the birds the way the old man seemed to.

"How did you learn to understand what they are saying?"

"You listen carefully, Carlos, and though you may also hear the whole universe around them, you must concentrate on their voices alone. This is the beauty and gift of listening."

The old man pointed to an eagle which landed on a nearby rock. Carlos watched the eagle as it took off to scour the countryside. The old man leaned forward and whispered into Carlos' ear.

"What is she saying, Carlos?"

Carlos could not hear the eagle say anything, but he did hear his heart speak.

This is my country. I am in love. Thank you for releasing me all those years ago in the mountains of Cyprus. See what I've become and done with my life. Don't you hear my brood in the trees above you?

Carlos was startled by the words his heart spoke. He listened again carefully.

I am the eagle. This is my place and I am proud to be here. I knew you'd find me again.

Carlos watched the eagle as it stretched its wings out as wide as it could and then launched itself into the air. He watched the magnificent creature riding the warm current and then glide away into the distant valley below. He knew he understood the eagle and the words she spoke.

The old man stood beside Carlos and raised both his arms to the heavens.

"What are you doing?"

"Now that you can truly listen, I'm summoning the light in your heart, Carlos."

Carlos smiled as he watched the figure of the old man with his outstretched arms against the rays of the setting sun. He could still feel the intense heat of the sun on his face and he noticed how heavily he had begun to perspire. The old man withdrew his arms from the heavens and turned to Carlos.

"Carlos...has your heart ever been broken in your life?"

Carlos was silent for a moment. It was as if his entire life flashed before his eyes. He thought about his parents and Monika.

"I don't know. I suppose it has. I mean, it must have been broken. I've lost both my parents to illness. I think of them every day and wish they were still here."

The old man did not answer, but Carlos heard him whisper something under his breath. At that moment, Carlos heard his heart speak again.

Love grows and flourishes in many different ways throughout our lives and it has many depths.

The old man bowed his head down and in an instant Carlos could feel a cool breeze rise. The light from the sun dimmed and he could see thick, menacing, grey clouds form across the sky. Carlos began to feel frightened. The old man lifted his head and looked across at Carlos.

Carlos remembered the advice Padre Callico had given him before he set out on his journey.

Use everything you are blessed with and believe in yourself and your instincts, and trade nothing on the road to Damascus.

"Old man, who are you?"

The old man smiled at Carlos.

"Carlos, hold your hands out as if you were about to catch something very precious."

Carlos held out his hands like the old man asked. Though he could see nothing in his hands, he felt the weight of something in his palms. The old man walked close to Carlos and whispered in his ear.

"You are holding your heart in your hands. Cherish it, and when others cherish it, you will eventually see your soul, but not until you are ready."

The old man gripped Carlos' hands and brought them firmly together.

"Keep what you hold dear and safe within your grasp. Give nothing up easily."

He pushed Carlos' cupped hands back against his chest.

"Who am I, or what am I? I'm the trees that hold the spirits of all who have loved you. I'm the happiness and fun in your life from the moment you open your eyes to the moment you sleep. I'm the scattering of light on a dull day and the blaze of sunshine in the middle of summer. I'm the long shadows in winter and what you see when the snowflakes melt. I'm the joy you'll feel when you're deeply in love and the empty arms you'll fall into when you're broken-hearted. I can be anything or anybody you want me to be; Saffri the fruit seller, Khaleb the truck driver, Ramon the Syrian farmer, Ahab the restaurant owner—I can even be Syam, the one who sent you away from your own village, or Bakkar. I can be all of them, but I will always be there."

Carlos looked at the old man in disbelief when he spoke. It was like someone had plundered his mind and heart of every memory and experience he ever had. He opened his palms and stared at his heart, and in that moment, though he still did not see his soul, he saw everything he loved and wished for in his life; right there, in the palm of his hands. His lifelines became every road he had walked upon, every river he had swam in, and every ring of growth from all the trees in the forests. He could see lines that had no end to them no matter how hard he looked. The old man pushed Carlos' hands towards his chest. He could feel the pressure almost pushing his whole body backwards.

Carlos tried to embrace the old man, but the old man gently pushed him away.

The old man raised his arms to the heavens once again, turned to Carlos, and smiled.

"Today, my name is Tass."

With that, he walked over to the edge of the precipice and pointed into the sky above Carlos' shoulder.

"Your eagle is calling to you, Carlos. See her before she leaves."

Carlos scanned the sky above, though he looked hard, he could not see her, but he was sure he could hear the whisper of a voice in the evening breeze.

Home.

When Carlos looked to the precipice, the old man was gone. He ran to the edge and looked everywhere but saw nothing only the mountainside stretch out below him. He wanted to call out, but could barely muster a faint whisper from his heart...

Tass!

Carlos reached the roadside. He looked in the direction of Damascus. Though he knew it wasn't far away, deep inside, he knew where he must go. He turned and began walking back home to Cyprus. He knew where to find Monika, and if she was no longer there, then he was happy to spend the rest of his life looking for her.

It was getting cool and Carlos dug his hands into his trouser pockets while he walked. He felt something and drew his right hand out and opened it. It was the sprig given to him by the old woman he had met in the city of Jerusalem. He had expected the sprig to be withered and broken after all these days, but there, lying in the palm of his hand was the most wonderful orchid bloom he had ever seen.

ABOUT THE AUTHOR

Mick Rooney is an author, researcher and freelance journalist. He has been writing for more than thirty years and published eleven books of fiction and non-fiction, including Filigree & Shadow, a collection of his shorter fiction. His debut novel was Academy.

He has written and published numerous articles in print and online over many years about publishing, music, aviation, translation and retail.

He was born in Dublin, Ireland in 1968 and now lives in the Netherlands.

Online & social media links

Website
www.mick-rooney.com
Twitter
@theindiepubmag
Facebook
www.facebook.com/MickRooneyAuthor/

www.ingramcontent.com/pod-product-compliance
Lightning Source LLC
Chambersburg PA
CBHW020418110726
47899CB00006B/2041